PASSAGE ON THE CARDENA

PASSAGE

── ON THE ──

CARDENA

A NOVEL BY MEL DAGG

TouchWood
Editions

TouchWood Editions
touchwoodeditions.com

LIBRARY AND ARCHIVES CANADA CATALOGUING IN PUBLICATION
Dagg, Mel, 1941–
Passage on the Cardena / Mel Dagg.

Also issued in electronic format.
ISBN 978-1-927129-33-3

I. Title.

PS8557.A3P38 2012   C813'.54   C2012-902548-8

Editor: Marlyn Horsdal
Proofreader: Sarah Weber
Design: Pete Kohut
Cover image: Cyril R. Littlebury *Union Steam Ship Co. ss Cardena*
Author photo: Lynne Dagg

We gratefully acknowledge the financial support for our publishing activities
from the Government of Canada through the Canada Book Fund, Canada
Council for the Arts, and the province of British Columbia through the
British Columbia Arts Council and the Book Publishing Tax Credit.

The interior pages of this book have been printed on 100% post-consumer
recycled paper, processed chlorine free, and printed with vegetable-based inks.

1   2   3   4   5   16   15   14   13   12

PRINTED IN CANADA

To Forrest Dagg

The company does not undertake to put passengers or freight on shore at destination, nor to call at any point when weather or other circumstances might cause danger or delay, nor to call at the ports in the order in which they are named.

I

A LOGGER BURST THROUGH THE swinging doors of Tommy Roberts's saloon, stumbled, and almost knocked over a boy on the sidewalk. The boy neatly sidestepped him and kept on walking. Sunday grey flannel pants and blue blazer, short blond hair perfectly parted, the boy looked lost and out of place on Vancouver's skid row.

Bent forward, intent, he turned left onto Carrall Street and walked across the railway tracks to where the street ended at the sea. He had followed his mother's directions to the Union Steamship dock. Something was wrong. His ship was not here. Was he lost? It wouldn't be the first time.

Matt's father worked as a logger and the family had lived in small towns on Vancouver Island, Parksville and Chemainus. The work was so dangerous that every day Frank Clayton went into the woods he risked his life. Finally, hoping he could find work safer than logging, Frank moved his family to Vancouver, but there was no work in the city and Frank had to return to what he knew, logging, this time farther up the coast, leaving Matt and his mother in Vancouver. In the city the boy often felt lost but this time it was serious. The ship he was supposed to sail on would leave without him.

He should have written his mother's directions on a piece of paper and carried them with him. Instead, he tried to remember, hearing again what she had said on the day she died.

> You must go into The Jungles and find your father. Not the tropics, but the rain forest where men like your father wrestle with trees and call it The Jungles. Listen carefully, I will tell you how to get there. Down Hastings, past Woodward's department store, in the block before Carrall you pass the Pantages Theatre. There's a trolley station on the southwest corner of Hastings and Carrall where the cars turn into the depot. You turn left and walk two blocks to your ship. The road ends at the foot of Carrall at the Union dock, the end of the road and the beginning of your journey.

He had done as she said. He was not lost. He simply could not find his ship. Traffic signs directed passengers who rushed past him, arriving and departing from the *Lady Cecilia*, the *Lady Alexandra*, the *Capilano II*, and the *Cardena*.

He stood at the wharf's main intersection and studied the signpost directory at its centre; the location on the pier of the ship's berth was indicated by an arrow and under the name of the ship its ports of call. The *Lady Pam* was there and under the sign pointing to her berth, a list of the *Pam*'s destinations: Gambier Island, Hopkins Landing, Port Mellon. The *Lady Evelyn*, the *Catala*, the *Camosun I*. Nowhere was the ship he had a ticket for, the *Venture*, listed.

Had his mother made a mistake? The last time he saw her alive, she couldn't lift her head from the pillow and he had to lean forward to hear her form words in a weak whisper. "You will live with your father now and to do that you must first find him."

He listened, amazed, while she told him she had passage for him on the *Venture* to Prince Rupert. She made it sound as if every day, a fifteen-year-old went up the coast on a steamer to find his father.

"What if I don't find him? What will happen to me?"

"Oh, you'll find him," she said. "People know your father on the coast."

Some flickering memory stirred in her. She lifted her head off the pillow but then began to sink back again, her eyes closing with a tired, faraway look that made him know, the instant they shut, she was dead.

He was alone, utterly alone.

He must not think of her now. He was lost at the edge of the sea, without a ship to sail on. He stood at the crossroad. The pier branched before him at right angles in four directions to different ships. Unable to find the *Venture*, he studied the directory again, taking note not just of each ship but its ports of call. Which ship, which journey? There were one hundred and sixty-five ports of call listed in the Union Steamship ABC Sailing Guide. In one of them, somewhere up the coast, he would find his father. He *must* find his father. He scanned the directory. SS *Cardena*: Campbell River, Alert Bay, Sointula, Prince Rupert, Skeena canneries, Anyox.

Walking down the dock toward the *Cardena*, on this August afternoon in 1930, he passed a small ship, grey-black smoke pouring from its funnel, as it came to berth. Girls in summer dresses and boys in bright whites clung to the ship's railing to watch the docking: the end of a perfect day. The summer gaiety of the picnickers and day trippers contrasted cruelly with the boy's growing despair.

He kept moving through the crowd toward the *Cardena*, concentrating on each step he must take to survive.

Winch men were working the freight booms that lifted cargo from the dock and lowered it into the *Cardena's* hold to the shouts and signals of longshoremen. Savory aromas wafted through the open porthole of the galley, reminding him that he had not eaten all day.

At the end of the pier, a heavy-set woman wearing a loose-fitting chocolate brown coat and cloche hat sat on a small canvas folding chair. A dog rested in her lap. Someone was taking her photograph.

The woman and her dog sat motionless, staring into the camera, the looped end of the dog's leash loose between her legs, its right forepaw resting on her knee. The woman's hat was pulled down so the brim almost hid her heavily shadowed eyes, her closed mouth set somewhere between a grimace and a smile for the camera. The shutter caught the moment, the woman and her dog stilled in time.

She relaxed her hold on the dog and it leapt from her lap, barking at the boy with all the bravado a small dog can muster.

"Harmless. Bark's worse than his bite. Rather like me. Or so my boarders tell me. They say I'm just like my dogs, snappy and cranky." The woman reined in the dog and stood up. "Hold his leash for a moment while I fold this chair."

"Can you tell me which ship goes to Prince Rupert?" asked Matthew, grasping the leash.

"Why, this very one," she said, turning toward the thick manila rope wrapped around the cleat on the dock, the bow of the ship looming above them. "The *Cardena*. It says so right there on the directory."

His fingers touched the ticket in his pants pocket, his single hope and only chance to find his father, a ticket fast becoming worthless. "Yes, I know. But my ticket says the ship is the *Venture*."

"Sometimes the company changes the ship. The important thing is to know where you are going. Where *are* you going?"

He didn't know where he was going because his father could be anywhere up the coast. Passengers rushed past him: families on summer excursions, Indian women with babies wrapped in wool shawls, loggers, gamblers, prospectors, promoters, students, Chinese cannery workers. Everyone knew where they were going except the boy, traumatized by the woman's question.

"I don't know really," he stammered. "You see I . . ."

He began telling her how his mother had died and left him to find his father somewhere up the coast, exactly where he didn't know because of the transient nature of his father's work as a logger, when the woman, seeing him on the verge of tears, interrupted.

"I think this is the boat you want because it's the one that will take you farthest up the coast."

But this didn't seem to ease the boy's grief, so she plunged on. "Being alone isn't so bad. My father died when I was in high school and my sisters and I have been on our own ever since. We're older than you but it's just the same."

"No. It's not the same. You have your sisters. You're not alone at all."

The woman looked at him through grey eyes. A whiner! No point telling him she had nothing in common with her sisters. They were from another planet, didn't even look like her. At the same age as this snivelling boy she had been a teenager living alone in a strange city, San Francisco.

But she wanted to make the boy feel better, not argue with him. "You're wrong. It *is* the same. No matter how many people are around, in the end, each of us is absolutely and completely alone. You just have to get used to it a little earlier than most of us. Living with yourself isn't so bad once you get to know who you are."

"Well that's easy. I know who I am."

"It's a lifetime's work. I'm still getting to know myself. It's not as easy as you might think. Do you see?"

"Sort of," he said, to be polite. "But how does a person get to know his self?"

"Everyone is different. The main thing is . . ."—her eyes dropped to the notebook in her lap—"I keep a journal. It's like having a conversation with yourself, or with a friend, except you write it down and then you can go back later and read it and reflect on it."

"May I see?"

Her hands held the journal's cover closed. "It's a private conversation." And not wanting to hurt the boy, she quickly added, "We'll be shipmates!" She paused to consider this. When she resumed, her voice took on a darker tone. "Well, for a while, anyway. I'm not going all the way to Prince Rupert. I'm getting off at Port Hardy. I must make the last part of my trip alone and, as I said, that's not so bad, being alone. Besides," she looked down at her dog, "I'll have Koko. That's his name. What's yours?"

"Matt . . . Matthew Clayton."

"When I was your age, my friends called me Millie, or Motor, and sometimes Carrlight. Car, like the automobile, only with two Rs, Carr. Emily Carr. This is your ship. I know it is."

The woman seemed very sure of herself, but one thing he

knew, his ticket was for the *Venture*, not the *Cardena*. It was all very confusing.

"THAT BOY IS lost," said one quartermaster to the other.

They were standing next to the boarding ramp on the *Cardena*, waiting for the first mate and captain to come aboard so they would know whose watch they would be on. In the meantime they leaned against the railing of the *Cardena*, watching the passengers on the dock below.

There were two kinds of passengers: those accompanied by family and friends, greeting or seeing them off, and those who were alone. Perhaps it was the solitary nature of a quartermaster's duties, standing at the wheel to steer the ship night and day, six hours on, six hours off, twelve hours a day, that made them notice the loners: the high rigger, tools in a canvas bag the weight of which he shifted from one shoulder to the other as he walked the wharf; a woman in long leather boots, legs crossed in a full pleated skirt, perched on a trunk in the middle of the bags and suitcases behind which she was barricading herself; and the boy who had been talking to the woman with the dog, the boy turning now to look up at the two men.

"Yes," agreed Paul Briggs, "he *is* lost."

"THAT'S MY HUSBAND supervising the loading of those crates." The woman spoke to the stranger with the easy familiarity of a fellow traveller. She wore a long blue gown that, from where Karl Pedersen stood behind her, clung uninvitingly to her thin frame when she stepped forward to wave at the small man in a suit and derby hat who stood on the dock staring at his pocket watch.

"Indeed!" replied Pedersen, knowing full well the only man who supervised any ship's business was the captain, or his officers acting on the captain's orders. "Is he, now!"

Stanley Shanks and his Swedish assistants, Einar and Ollie Gunderson, stood by while the *Cardena*'s winch man worked the freight boom. It was loading six wooden crates containing machinery the salesman and the two Swedes planned to demonstrate in settlements and camps up the coast.

Stanley's eyes followed each crate as it was lifted from the wharf, swung onto the *Cardena*'s forward deck, and lowered into the hold. He was timing the loading of the crates with his pocket watch. Everything—his life, his future—was contained in those crates.

Stanley had wanted his crates to remain on deck to facilitate speedy access, the unloading and assembly at each stop along the *Cardena*'s route where the demonstrations were to be staged, but the deck crew had argued against this, citing heavy seas in which the crates could shift, and if the forward deck flooded, the crates could be damaged.

So Shanks had deferred to their good sense. It was, after all, not his ship. As a compromise, they had agreed, just as Stanley was now witnessing, to load the six crates last. Then, at each stop, his crates would be first out of the hold, thereby giving him and his assistants half an hour to set up and forty-five minutes for the demonstration, minus, of course, the time needed to unload and load the crates back onboard, which Stanley was now timing.

The *Cardena*'s freight boom lifted the last crate from the Union wharf, swung it onto the ship's deck, and lowered it into the hold.

Stanley snapped his pocket watch shut and turned to his

assistants. "Exactly five minutes and thirty seconds to load our crates. Say it takes the same time to unload that it takes to load, so multiply by two, and that's eleven minutes off our allotted ninety minutes to unpack, set up, give our demonstration, pack up, and load the crates back onboard the *Cardena*."

He paused for a moment to allow them to digest these calculations.

"Time, gentleman," intoned Stanley. "Never neglect the time factor." It excited him to think he was on the outer wave of change and that his machine, the device he would demonstrate, would be the instrument of that change.

The two Swedes he had hired out of the Exeter Hotel on Vancouver's east side stared at him blankly. They hadn't the slightest idea what Stanley was talking about.

Some of the limited English the Swedes knew consisted of the rhyme they had memorized to guide them on their way when they landed on the east coast and rode the rails west, looking for a job in the woods:

Vancouver,
CPR,
Tommy Roberts,
Cassiar

Tommy Roberts ran a hiring hall in his Grand Hotel where you could get a job in the camps up the coast, and the *Cassiar* was the Union steamship that took you there. The ship had come out of Wallace Shipbuilders in False Creek in 1901, but it was built on the hull of a schooner launched in 1890, and the retrofitted cabin work didn't quite fit the lines of the hull. It was called "the logger's palace"; caulk boots could be worn on deck, the bar never closed, and it had an onboard jail.

Einar Gunderson scanned the wharf in vain for the *Cassiar*'s blunt-nosed chunky form. "We ain't loadin' these crates on the *Cassiar*!"

The Swedes locked eyes and then Ollie looked up at the sleek lines of the Union's flagship. Through its portholes he glimpsed waiters fussing over tables as they set out silverware on linen table-cloths in the dining room.

"Ya, Einar! Dis ain't da *Cassiar*. Dat's for sure!"

STANDBY, SIGNALLED THE jingling telegraph in the *Cardena*'s engine room. The ship's twin triple-expansion steam engines hissed and throbbed. The muffled voices of men loading freight came from deep within the ship's hold. The pulse of steam. The crew, the lights, the ship coming to life.

THE HIGH RIGGER walked the length of the wharf, waiting to board the *Cardena*. He passed a gang of Chinese cannery workers, an Indian family, some loggers who acknowledged him with a nod.

The woman watched him walk by, his back to her. There was something wild and feral about him, and it was this, though she didn't know it, that interested her. He was, she decided, an alien here in the city who would be at home only in the woods, a place she herself had never been.

He reached the end of the dock and turned, and as he began walking toward her, she saw him more closely. He wore a plain olive green mackinaw, gabardine slacks, a tan wool shirt, and no hat, his blond hair short and unruly. There was a familiarity about him she couldn't quite place.

"A fellow passenger," she blurted, "if I'm not mistaken. Passengers?" she repeated, craving company, for he had turned away. "We are passengers on the *Cardena*."

Cameron turned to the pleasant feminine voice calling to him from behind some luggage, saw her face, round and full, her hair upswept, green eyes staring at him, and then, instinctively, he turned away. She was beautiful.

"Not quite yet," he said, his eyes following the line on the dock to the bow of the ship that loomed above them. "They're still loading."

A horse in a huge pen was being lifted from the dock to the ship. Someone had put blinders on the animal, and its nostrils flared and snorted as it shook its mane from side to side.

"Soon," said the woman, as much to reassure herself as to address the solitary man who seemed to be avoiding her.

THE EXCITEMENT ON the dock was palpable. Passengers about to board the *Cardena* were pressing forward to the gangway, as the last of the crew arrived. Ships' officers in dark navy blue coats moved single file up the gangway.

Honking constantly to clear a path, a taxi slowly made its way down the wharf.

"The *Cardena*, as usual?" The driver eyed his passenger in the mirror and the old man slumped in the backseat nodded his assent.

"I'll get an update on your return time and be waiting for you at the dock. Have a good trip, sir."

"Yes, Raymond. I believe I will."

Already he could hear the music, the band playing in the lounge. He closed his eyes and saw the people standing on the wharf in every cove and inlet where his ship would stop. Boat Day. People waiting on the dock for the ship to bring them mail, freight, provisions, relatives returning from Vancouver. Faces he had come to know over the years looking up to him on the bridge to bring the ship to them, manoeuvring it—their lifeline to the outside world—in to the dock. He wouldn't let them down, and when they got to Port Hardy they'd play a Saturday night dance for the town.

The cab pulled up to the *Cardena*'s boarding ramp and the driver stepped out to open the door for his fare. The white-haired elderly man stooped to clear the cab doorway, his hat in his hand, and then, straightening, stared up at the *Cardena* rising above him. He looked at the ship for what seemed a very long time, standing on the dock in an old, crumpled navy blue uniform. He placed his cap on his head and, grasping the side rope to steady himself, slowly began making his way up the gangplank.

The cab driver did not start the engine and drive from the dock but instead sat behind the steering wheel, watching the old man's slow progress. He considered the captain his personal charge and would not leave the dock until he saw him safely onboard the *Cardena*.

He had a standing order to pick up the captain every Friday and drive him to the Union dock. For four years, the same cab driver had been coming to his door at seven thirty on Friday evenings.

He used to wait in front of the house while the captain said his final farewells to his wife. The two of them embraced on the front porch and sometimes she would walk him to the cab, Boyce wearing a double-breasted captain's jacket with two rows of brass buttons and four gold stripes on the sleeves, a white, black-peaked captain's hat tucked under his arm, and trousers pressed sharp as a razor.

Not now. Not since his wife's death. Now, when Raymond pulled up to the captain's house, Boyce was never ready and, after waiting a requisite fifteen minutes, Raymond would begin honking his horn. What's he doing in there? he worried. It was almost as if, since his wife's death, Boyce used the arrival of the cab as the signal that it was time to go and then would make the cab wait while he got ready. Finally, half an hour later, a crumpled and beleaguered figure would emerge from the house.

Raymond watched the old man step safely onboard the *Cardena*. The crew would look after him now. The cabbie started his motor and drove from the dock.

"IS THAT HIM?"

"Just now coming aboard," replied Mike Wilson, an old hand who had sailed with Captain Boyce many times.

The old man steadied himself on the gangplank, his hat so askew on his head that the peak pointed sideways.

"What's he like?" Paul Briggs was a newcomer who had gotten the quartermaster job through contacts. This was his first trip out and he was nervous. Wilson sensed this and decided to have some fun.

"Wait until you're in fog in the Narrows with Captain Jack," he said. "Then you'll see."

"What do you mean?"

"Thicker the better," said Wilson, piling it on. "The fog, that is. Fog's what he likes best. They call him the Fog Wizard. Does the whole thing with his eyes closed. Listening to the echo off the ship's whistle."

He watched the younger man shift his feet and push against the rail as if thinking to jump down onto the safety of the dock. Wilson had him now. It was great fun.

"To help him concentrate," added Wilson. "Keeping his eyes closed, I mean."

Boyce knew the two quartermasters were talking about him and when he finally got to the top of the ramp he turned and faced them.

"Gentlemen," he said, nodding to them. He reached into his pocket and removed a silver dollar. "Who will have the pleasure of taking us out of port tonight? Which quartermaster will stand watch with their captain?"

Boyce tossed the coin and as it spun in the air Wilson remained silent. It was all the same to him. He didn't care which watch he took. The skipper was all right with him.

"Tails!" called Briggs, his eye following the coin as it clattered onto the deck.

Heads. He had lost.

My God! He was shipping out with someone who was going to take a steamship through Seymour Narrows with his eyes closed, listening for echoes.

"TICKETS, PLEASE. TICKETS."

The boy handed his ticket to the purser who examined it and said, "This ticket's for the *Venture*. Where'd you get this ticket, son?"

"My mother. Is something the matter?"

"No, no. Perfectly all right. Perfectly good ticket."

The purser flipped it in his fingers, turning it over.

He handed Matthew back his portion of the ticket. "Welcome aboard the *Cardena*, son."

"Thank you."

He was halfway up the gangway between the dock and the ship when it hit him. He was sailing on his mother's ticket. It was not his ticket but a ticket she had bought when the *Venture* was on the Prince Rupert run, a ticket she had decided, for some reason, not to use. The ramp seemed to sway beneath him. He grabbed the guide rope for support, his feet missing the ramp's wooden cleats.

"Are you all right, Matthew?"

The voice behind him sounded like his mother's but then he realized it was the Carr woman. "I'm all right," he answered, without turning around. "I just lost my footing."

Then he heard his mother's voice, clear as if she was alive and walking behind him.

"You must get up, you know. You are all we've got left, your father and I. Now get up and go find your father."

"RELEASE THE BOW!"

From the bridge Boyce watched a man on the dock lift the looped end of a steel cable off a bollard and drop it into the water with a loud smack; hand over hand, two deckhands pulled the heavy cable onboard.

Boyce reached behind him to operate the brass handle of the ship's telegraph so he could, at the same moment, look over the bridge, keeping watch always on his ship and the dock during his manoeuvres.

He moved the handle, operating the telegraph by feel, for as the hand behind his back moved the handle, his thumbnail trailed across the notched brass dial, counting, counting, and stopped: a jingle and two gongs, Slow Astern. The telegraph rang and was answered from the engine room. The ship moved astern against a back spring line, helm over, causing the bow to swing out from the dock.

He was all right now that he was at the controls. A day's damp sea air would take the crumple out of his uniform. He had no life on land; the life he had always looked forward to at the end of every trip, to come home to his wife, Edith, was over. When she was alive, she had been his whole reason for completing the trip. Now that she was gone, the trip had become an end in itself. Yes, he thought, his hand working the telegraph as the bow of his ship swung out from the dock, he still had the *Cardena*. He was master of the flagship of the fleet.

THOUGH THE *CARDENA* was scheduled to leave Vancouver at nine thirty, it had been late loading and late departing. Passengers were gathering along the port deck to witness the departure, the steamship illuminated in the lights of the city's harbour. Small boys climbed to the middle rail and, holding fast to the top one, hung out over it, enthralled, staring down at the sea below.

The passengers gazed at the city sliding by them in the night. It was beautiful but there was a profound, haunting loneliness about it too.

On the forward deck a trio of loggers with a bottle was joined by the two Swedes, Einar and Ollie. One of the loggers called across the deck to the lone man at the railing. "Hey, Will. Will Cameron.

We got the good stuff here." The logger waved the bottle over his head. "How about it?"

"No thanks."

Cameron moved away from his fellow loggers to the afterdeck, preoccupied with his own thoughts. In Vancouver, earlier in the day, he had purchased ten acres on an island off the northern end of Vancouver Island that he was anxious to see. He was going to a high-rigging job out of Port Hardy so he wouldn't see the land right away, but when he finished the job, he could hire a fisherman to take him there.

Cameron was lost in these thoughts when he heard the voice of the woman who had spoken to him on the dock.

She was standing beside him at the railing. "It's an act of faith, really. Putting to sea. Cut loose from the moorings. That sort of thing. There's a freedom in it, don't you think?"

"Are you asking me what I think about freedom?" He looked down from the main deck into the churn of eddying water, the backwash from the *Cardena* trailing behind the stern into the receding lights of the city.

"Yes, I am."

But it was herself she was trying to convince of the freedom of the voyage, for she was not free but someone's mistress. At the end of the *Cardena's* voyage and at the end of a long, narrow inlet, the manager of a copper mine waited for her, an older man who would bully and dominate her. And so she had decided that for these last few days at sea she *would* be free.

"Yes. Yes, I am. It's wonderful, this sense of freedom. Exhilarating. Like the sea air." Yes, I am free, she thought to herself.

Her eyes were pale green, cat's-eye green, flecked with grey and brown, like sand mingling with the Pacific Ocean at the mouth of the Fraser or Capilano River where the water is always shifting colour, the very water the *Cardena* was now moving through; just so, her eyes were changing colour.

But at night no one could see the colour of the water, nor how long the moment between the man and the woman lasted: seconds, though in memory, forever, this moment of recognition, the discovery of seeing each other for the first time.

And what, Cameron wondered, looking into her green eyes, does she see in me?

Just then the steward was making his rounds as the ship slipped through First Narrows. "First call! First call to dinner!" he shouted.

"It's true I have not shaved for two days but my thoughts are pure. Would you join me for dinner?"

"No, your thoughts are not pure. And yes," she hooked her arm in his, "I would very much like to dine with you."

MATTHEW MOVED OUT of the press of passengers on the promenade deck, grasped the outer railing for support, and stared blankly back at the city he was leaving. He knew now. He was sailing on his mother's ticket. It was not his ticket. It never had been. She had saved it for herself to go visit his father, and then, for some reason, she hadn't. Something had happened between his mother and father that he didn't know about.

Since his mother's death three days ago, he hadn't stopped moving, and now, standing at the ship's railing as the *Cardena* left Vancouver, he saw for the first time where he truly was, in a black void deep as the dark water below him. He stared overboard into the whirling water streaming by the ship. No one would know if he jumped. The ship would go on. Would he even be missed? Who would miss him?

Astern of the ship, the lights of the city diminished in the growing distance, the city where he and his uncle and aunt had buried his mother, the city where there was nothing left for him to return to now she was gone. And ahead? Where was the *Cardena* taking him? Into an unknown world where his only hope was to find his father.

"Bong, bing, bing, ting, bing, bong!" The steward's dinner chime broke into his thoughts. The steward wore a white coat and black bow tie, and punctuated his announcement on a musical chime: "First call! First call to dinner!"

"Are you hungry, Matt?" It was the Carr woman. "Matthew?"

He nodded his head, fighting back tears, still struggling with the puzzle of the ticket and how to begin the search for his father. "Yes. Of course I am."

"If we hurry we can make the first sitting," Emily said, and pulled him by his jacket to the purser's office to purchase meal tickets.

They descended the stairs to the dining room where a waiter took their dinner tickets and showed them to a table at which a couple was already seated.

Matt placed his hands on the back of Emily's chair to move it for her before she sat down but it wouldn't budge. The table and chairs had been bolted to the floor in case of rough seas. Emily gave her coat and hat to the steward and sat down next to Matt. She wore a hairnet with a wide velvet band across her broad forehead.

Matt, Emily, and the other couple studied the menu, a complicated document, the cover decorated with a coastal scene, a Union steamship in the foreground. What, Matt wondered, was Veal Fricassee? And why would anyone want to eat Sardines on Toast, or Iced Green Olives?

Matt had all but given up on the menu when the man seated across from him said, "The lamb's very good. They always serve it on the first night out."

"You must make this trip often," said the woman seated next to him.

"Whenever they need a high rigger."

Matt dropped his menu onto the table, no longer interested in it. He knew what a high rigger was from listening to his father. "Do you know my father, Frank Clayton?"

"Matt is trying to find his father," broke in Emily.

"No. Can't say as I do," replied the high rigger.

The waiter came and took their orders. They were all ordering lamb except the woman with the high rigger.

"I'd like the ling cod with parsley sauce."

"I'm sorry," apologized the waiter. "I'm afraid it's not available this evening."

"Very well. I'll try the boiled ox heart with the Italian sauce."

The waiter took away their menus and left them in the awkward silence of strangers.

Still, Emily told herself, it could be worse, much worse. The *Cardena*'s dining room was always filled for the first sitting, and if you were travelling alone, you got thrown in with the trash and misfits. Once, on this very same ship, they had seated her at a table with a passed-out drunk who snored and slobbered on the tablecloth while she tried to eat her dinner. No, this wasn't so bad, she thought, looking across the table at the high rigger and a woman in her late thirties who was still beautiful but already fading; in the politest of terms an adventuress, here on this final frontier. Surely she was not travelling with this logger, and yet they seemed so infatuated with each other, Emily could hardly bear to look at them.

"Are you travelling far?" Emily asked.

"Far as this ship will take me," said the woman. "To the copper mine at Anyox." She passed a bowl of dinner rolls across the table and, as Emily took it, said, "My name's Monica James."

"Cameron," said the man beside Monica James. "William Cameron. And you?"

"Emily. Emily Carr."

"Where are you going?"

"I'm getting off at Port Hardy."

"Whatever for?" asked Cameron. "What's in Port Hardy?"

"Nothing. Absolutely nothing. But it's where my real trip begins." She could not tell these strangers that she was about to embark on a journey she had been preparing for all her life, so she said, "I will hire a small boat to take me around the northern tip of Vancouver Island and up Quatsino Sound."

Cameron had once taken the same trip himself and was now more puzzled than ever. Why was this elderly lady travelling alone into the wilderness?

"Be careful who you hire. The open sea gets nasty off Cape Scott."

It was customary to serve dinner late on the first night out from

Vancouver, and all four were now so hungry that when their dinners arrived, conversation momentarily ceased.

"THIS . . ." MARTHA SHANKS'S bejewelled fingers and polished nails swirled above her head in a flourish that took in the entire dining room: the maple veneer, the ornate columns, the beautifully crafted chairs, a napkin folded to a peak in front of her and, at every place setting, sterling silver cutlery and china embossed with the Union Steamship logo. "It's quite fantastic. Not a ferry service at all. More like a luxury liner. Why, the only thing missing," another wave of her hand, "is a chandelier."

"Not a good idea," said Karl Pedersen who had joined Stanley and Martha Shanks's table. He could not resist the Shankses, convinced by everything Martha Shanks had told him that her husband was a perfect prospect for Pedersen's mining stock.

"Can you imagine a chandelier when a ship is in rough seas? No. Not a good idea at all."

"Rough seas? Surely not in our famed Inside Passage, Mr. Pedersen."

"Yes. The Inside Passage. Straits created by the great islands that lie just off our coast, the Queen Charlottes in the north and Vancouver Island in the south. Imagine your Inside Passage as the shape of an hourglass." Pedersen used both his hands to shape an hourglass.

Stanley envisioned Pedersen's hourglass as the shape of a woman, not his wife, more like the woman seated at the table next to them with the boy, the older woman, and another man.

"Georgia and Queen Charlotte straits at either end narrowing, pinched into the constricted passage of Seymour Narrows."

Pedersen's hands shaped the hourglass a second time for emphasis.

"The tidal stream enters around the north end of Vancouver Island and flows down Queen Charlotte and Johnstone straits. Are you following me, Mrs. Shanks?"

"Perfectly," replied Martha Shanks, annoyed by Pedersen's pedantry. "I am following both you *and* the flow of the water you are describing."

"All that water is pinched in the hourglass and boils through the great rapids of Seymour Narrows on the flood. Off Cape Mudge, Discovery Pass is like a wide, swift river, and in that swift water a southeast blow can rear up in a short high sea that has sunk more than one vessel."

"Sunken ships? In the sheltered water between Vancouver Island and the mainland? Surely you exaggerate, Mr. Pedersen."

"Don't take my word for it, madam. We'll be there before morning and you can judge for yourself."

Martha Shanks's mouth fell open. "You mean . . ." she began to stammer.

"Yes. Before morning we will be in that very body of water I speak of, but allow me to correct myself. We will be *on* the water, not in it. In matters marine the distinction between on and in can be the difference between life and death."

Martha looked across the table at her husband, her face filled with the realization, perhaps for the first time, of where she was and the nature of the voyage she had embarked on.

It was Stanley who had talked her into accompanying him on the trip north. Why not, she thought, when she heard about the scenery on the voyage. After all, it was her inheritance that was financing Stanley's latest venture, his machine that would revolutionize logging.

"This is huge, Martha," Stanley had told her. "Huge. The chance of a lifetime. You've got to see it."

The china rattled and jiggled on the table in front of her.

"Just a little southeaster," said Pedersen. "I have every confidence in Captain Boyce."

Martha Shanks's hand shook so badly she couldn't lift her cup. She watched her tea slop over the edge into the saucer and wished she'd stayed at home.

CAMERON SPREAD SOME mint jelly on a piece of lamb, speared it with his fork, and watched the boy across from him wipe his plate clean with a bread roll.

"Just because I've never met your father doesn't mean he's not up this coast somewhere. They only use a high rigger like me when they need a spar tree topped and rigged in the bigger shows. If he's working for some gyppo outfit with an A-frame on a raft, pulling logs off a hillside into the water, well, I wouldn't have run into him, but one thing's sure . . ."

The boy swallowed the last of his bun and looked at Cameron. "What's that?"

"If your father's logging on this coast, he's been on the *Cardena*, and even if he hasn't been on it for a while, this ship has probably hauled supplies in to him. Boom chains, cable, machinery, grub—the *Cardena*'s a lifeline for those little outfits. It's their only contact with the outside world. If I were you, I'd start talking to the crew. They might know something.

"Another thing. There are a dozen scheduled stops on this route and plenty more that aren't. Every place the *Cardena* docks, you should ask Captain Boyce how much time he'll take to unload and load and spend that time ashore asking after your father, even if it's only half an hour or twenty minutes. We make our first stop tomorrow. Campbell River. I'll go with you, if you like. We'll ask around."

Matt stared at his plate. He had cleaned it so thoroughly it almost sparkled, and there, embossed in its centre, was the Union Steamship logo: a barometer with the needle set on fair weather encircled by the words NORTH BY WEST IN THE SUNLIGHT. "Thank you," he said. He was no longer alone. He looked into the pleasant round face of the woman who had befriended him, her headband stretched across her forehead, unruly wisps of grey hair tufting over each ear.

Emily gazed at Matt with her contemplative grey eyes. Surely, she thought, if his father had wanted to be found, he would have made himself known to the boy. She didn't have the heart to tell him the simple truth that even Cameron, who was trying to be so helpful, must have guessed, the simple truth no one had yet confronted. The boy had become an orphan.

II

UNABLE TO SLEEP AND WANTING to explore the ship, Matt made his way down to that part of the ship below deck designated off limits to passengers, the engine room. At the centre of a maze of pipes, valves, boilers, and bearings, a red-faced man in white coveralls sat in a padded wicker chair, wiping his brow with a handkerchief and dabbing at his neck.

The chief engineer was sweating the alcohol out of his system; the temperature in the engine room was 110 degrees Fahrenheit. Archie Mackinnon had come aboard so drunk he had to be helped up the gangway and the second engineer had had to take the *Cardena* out of Vancouver.

Now Mackinnon was sober, drinking black coffee, and so attuned to his twin triple-expansion engines that he could sense the slightest alteration in their performance by the change of air in the engine room. One thing he was certain of, the control and running of the ship was in his hands.

Except for the steering of the ship by the quartermaster, there were no direct controls in the wheelhouse. Changes in the ship's speed—Slow, Half, Full—and changes in the ship's direction—Astern, Ahead—were all effected by the engineer at his controls in the engine room.

Connecting rods on each of the three pistons on the twin engines moved up and down on either side of where Matt and the chief sat in the centre of the ship's throbbing energy.

"Make no mistake," said the chief, dabbing at droplets of sweat forming on his forehead. "We run the ship down here. This is where it all happens."

"What about the ship's telegraph in the wheelhouse?" challenged Matt.

"The name says it all, doesn't it? Telegraph. It's not a control, just a device so the captain can tell me what he wants me to do. Then, when they mess up, take out a wharf while docking, for instance, they blame us. 'I rang for Full Astern,' they'll say, 'but the chief gave me Full Ahead.' No, son, this is where we control the ship."

"Well then," said Matthew. "What *does* the captain do?"

The chief poured black coffee from a battered tin Thermos into a grease-smudged cup and passed it to the boy. Matthew lifted the cup to his lips, looked across the blue oil that skimmed its surface, and waited for the engineer's answer.

"He squires ladies around the promenade deck on his arm and shows them how to play shuffleboard."

"I'LL BE IN the chart room," Boyce told his new quartermaster and stepped out of the wheelhouse to leave Briggs alone at the wheel in the dark. Except for giving him a course to steer by, these were the only words the captain had spoken to Briggs since they had left Vancouver.

Boyce pulled the chain on the lamp over the chart table. Under the table were trays of nautical charts that, if placed end to end, would make up a gigantic map of the Inside Passage, the narrow body of water between Vancouver Island and the mainland of North America.

The length of Vancouver Island was some five hundred miles measured as a straight line, but Boyce knew there was not a straight stretch of coastline anywhere, only a maze of coves, inlets, and bays so convoluted it actually comprised seventeen thousand miles. Boyce studied the charts showing the nooks and crannies he would take the *Cardena* into, tiny settlements waiting for their only connection to the outside world. Then, at the northern end of the trip, he would navigate his ship up the Skeena River to twelve salmon canneries. He accomplished all this by keeping a scrupulously detailed logbook, maintaining a consistent speed, and possessing the uncanny ability to read the echo off the ship's whistle.

It is all there on the charts, he thought, every reef, every shallow, every hazard. But no chart can explain fog so thick a searchlight cannot penetrate it; the sucking whirlpools and eddies of Seymour Narrows; the deadly sound of a steel hull on a hard rock hidden just below the surface; the screech of steel that produced sheer terror while you held your breath and prayed you would scrape over it clear.

What chart, he wondered, remembering only three years ago, the humiliation still fresh in his mind, could possibly foresee a storm so strong it moved a marker buoy? It was the worst disaster of his career, losing the *Catala*, the *Cardena*'s sister ship, on the route south from Port Simpson to Prince Rupert. The approach to Sparrowhawk Reef in Finlayson Channel was supposed to be marked by a buoy but a storm the night before had broken it free, pushed it across the channel, and wedged it on the reef.

His chief officer, a fool named Saunders, didn't notice the marker had moved and ran the ship aground onto the rocks of Sparrowhawk Reef, and then, worse still, lied about it. Said he wasn't on watch, wasn't in the wheelhouse, wasn't on the bridge. He thought the skipper, Boyce, was on the bridge and had taken over.

Boyce took the rap, even though when the ship went aground, he was nowhere near the bridge but back of the wheelhouse watering his little garden of pink geraniums and white carnations. The ship hit the reef with such force it sent him, his watering can, and the flower boxes skidding across the upper deck.

Horrible to see, the *Catala* high and dry on that reef and then, when the tide began to drop, the ship tilting over on its side, its hull naked and exposed. A humiliating disgrace made worse by the indignity of a marine inquiry.

"Now, Captain Boyce, you have heard Chief Officer Saunders testify he was not on the bridge when the *Catala* went aground, and further, that he saw you, Captain Boyce, on the bridge and so assumed you'd taken over. Is this what happened? Can you give us your version of events?"

Suddenly Boyce understood that the true meaning and purpose of the marine inquiry was not to determine the truth of what had happened or who was to blame. No, it was an inquiry into a man's character. He had listened to Saunders's testimony and heard, beneath the mask of the efficient sailor, a poor, frightened man prepared to lie to save his career.

Boyce stood up and faced them. The whole crew knew Saunders had been in the wheelhouse when they went aground, not Boyce, and now they waited for him to testify and refute the lie.

"Well," Boyce said, "if First Officer Saunders thinks I took over, I guess I must have taken over."

That was all he had to say. He took the fall. It wasn't worth lowering himself to play their game. It was time to abandon ship, which was exactly what happened when Saunders put the *Catala* aground on Sparrowhawk Reef. She lay stranded there on her side for a month, wouldn't budge; they couldn't get her off the rocks with towboats. Then a hardrock miner who knew nothing about boats but all about dynamite said, "I'll get her off. I'll blow the bugger off."

Boyce grabbed the miner by the rough wool of his Stanfields and shook him hard. "Don't you *ever* call my ship that again or it's *you* who'll be buggered!"

But the powder man set the charges in the rock under her hull and dynamited the *Catala* free off Sparrowhawk Reef. It was no way to treat a lady. Blast a hole in her hull, then patch it, refloat and tow her to Vancouver Drydock for repair. The *Catala* was in a huge pen, the sea water pumped out until the pen was dry and the hull bare and accessible below the waterline, a system of blocks all that kept the ship upright and prevented her from toppling over.

A ship out of water was a ship in disgrace; the white enamel and woodwork of the cabins were coated with grimy bunker fuel leaked from punctured tanks. The reef had torn the hull as if it were paper, ripping large square sheets of iron plate out along the popped rivet lines in a gaping hole so big Boyce could see into the hold of the ship.

He had never seen his ship look so vulnerable. A ship was only as good as its crew, and the crew had not been good enough. When

Boyce saw the *Catala* on blocks in drydock, something happened to him, something he couldn't explain. He felt he had let his ship down, lost her. He had come to know an old truth, that a sailor without a ship or a captain without a command was nothing.

Saunders never showed his face again after his false testimony, and Boyce began to hand pick a new crew, scrutinizing each man closely. If a ship was only as good as its crew, he wanted the best.

While the drydock workers repaired the hull and the shipwrights straightened a bent shaft and an out-of-balance propeller, Boyce was given command of the *Catala*'s sister ship, the *Cardena*.

In the years after the Sparrowhawk Reef disaster, Boyce began to define what he wanted the *Cardena* to be, transforming her so that she took on aspects and features of a ship larger than she actually was. He made the *Cardena* the most civilized, safest, and most elegant ship on the coast. On-deck shuffleboard, a lounge, complete dining service, and best of all, an onboard band, the Musical Mariners. They could be up some remote channel, mountains dropping straight down into the sea on either side of the ship, but by God, music would echo off those mountains, and on Saturday night they would play a dance in Port Hardy.

There would always be another Sparrowhawk Reef waiting to test him. You were never far from land on the Inside Passage, whether it was on the charts or it popped up unexpectedly, hidden just under the water, waiting to rip into the hull. It was inevitable. It was the nature of the coast. Tomorrow, beyond Campbell River, the seething water of Seymour Narrows would break over Ripple Rock.

Boyce finished his calculations and turned off the lamp over the chart table. If they left Campbell River on time, they would make the slack tide in the Narrows and arrive at Port Hardy on schedule. He walked out of the chart room into the wheelhouse and stood behind the quartermaster.

"Bring her round slowly," said Boyce. "North by West."

"North by West," repeated Briggs and began slowly turning the wheel in small increments, his eyes on the moving compass points.

The new quartermaster had become unnerved by the absence of the captain from the wheelhouse but, now that Boyce had returned, the tension in his outstretched arms and his hands on the wheel relaxed.

THE SEA BROKE white and curling from the *Cardena*'s bow, streaming along her sides and converging at her stern, where Monica and Cameron watched it trail in the distance behind them.

"It'll get rough tonight," said Cameron. "Just a light chop now but when it starts to break at the peaks . . ."

"Shh," Monica whispered, pressing herself hard against him. "Don't say a thing."

As if he could, he thought, mutter anything but inanities about the weather and the sea to this beautiful woman, and so he didn't, letting her lead him by the hand to her cabin.

MONICA'S BREASTS MOVED to the rocking motion of the ship as she sat naked, legs crossed on the small bed in her cabin. Cameron was overwhelmed, impotent.

"I'm sorry."

"Please stay. We have all night."

"Yes," he said, moving toward her.

HE WAS ALL right around others, or so Matt thought, seeking the company of Boyce and Briggs in the wheelhouse, Mackinnon down in the engine room, putting on a brave face for the passengers and crew, not letting his sorrow show, busy in the moment, relating to others.But when he was alone, as when Emily had come upon him earlier that evening, the knowledge of where he truly was overwhelmed him.

Sometime past midnight on his first night out of port, Matt put in place the sideboard of his bunk to prevent himself from falling out during rough seas. Even if the sea had been calm, he knew he was in for a sleepless night of troubling thoughts.

Since his mother's death, he'd had no time to grieve, and now, as he lay in his bunk in the darkness of the forecastle, her memory flooded in upon him, and with it, utter hopelessness. He slipped momentarily into a state of denial. He had been certain he heard his mother's voice when he was boarding the *Cardena*, but it was no use. She was gone and he was alone, encapsulated in the steel hull of a ship churning through the night.

Not much money left, a few dollar bills, some change. Suppose he didn't find his father. What in the world would happen to him?

He turned on his side and listened to the sea rush against the hull. He couldn't sleep; he sat up and stared out the porthole of his port side cabin at Vancouver Island. The *Cardena* was steaming up the strait at a full sixteen knots. He could see the lights of Parksville, but the village where he had lived now seemed thousands of miles away. Then the *Cardena* passed Qualicum. Any passengers still awake on the starboard side saw the humped, huge form of Texada Island silhouetted in the night.

The southeaster that earlier in the evening had merely rattled Martha Shanks's teacup was now a full-force gale. The wide, swift current of Discovery Pass poured into the gulf, combining with the southeast blow to rear up in a high sea off Cape Mudge.

FROM THE HEIGHT of the bridge Boyce and the quartermaster watched the bow of their ship bury itself and then rise again, the sea flooding the forward deck. Each of them held onto some part of the wheelhouse to prevent themselves being pitched across as the waves slammed against the *Cardena* and spun the quartermaster's compass points to a blur.

Briggs held onto the wheel with both hands and waited for the next ascent. The bow of the *Cardena* shot up out of the sea and he braced himself for the full jarring force of smashing down into it again. Each time the bow of the ship slammed into the sea and then back up out of it, he felt the layers inside his head separate and come together again.

DREAMING OF MONICA JAMES, Stanley Shanks awoke with an erection that quickly subsided at the sight of his wife on her knees, her head in the toilet bowl.

"I am not," she gasped, between spasms of heaving that shook her thin frame, "a well person."

"Pedersen warned you about Cape Mudge but you wouldn't listen," said Stanley. "If you hadn't had that dessert . . ."

He himself had never been seasick in his life but of one thing he was certain. If he didn't get out of the close quarters of their cabin, now filled with the smell of his wife's vomit, he would be very ill indeed.

"I'm going to the bar to check on Einar and Ollie."

"I will never, *ever* forgive you for this."

Stanley dressed quickly, shut the cabin door and made his way down the tilting, flooded, outside deck, then opened a door to the bar inside.

"I SAY, OLD boy!" Pedersen looked down at Stanley's soaked pant cuffs, pools of sea water forming at his shoes. "Rough weather?"

Stanley knew very well Pedersen wasn't referring to the weather, for why would a married man leave the comfort of his cabin at such a late hour? "Rather," he replied.

"In that case," said Pedersen, "let me buy you a drink."

The two men fell to talking of the economy and the depression then ravaging the country and driving most men to despair. Pedersen spoke in confident clichés, choosing his words carefully to include Stanley.

"For men such as ourselves, men who can see into the future, men who are ahead of our time, this depression is merely an opportunity to get in now on the ground floor. Do you see?"

Never had Stanley heard a man exude the confidence of Pedersen. The very fact that he was included in such a conversation bolstered Stanley's own sense of confidence.

"Yes, I do," lied Stanley. "But . . ."

"Oh, I know," interrupted Pedersen. "To take advantage, to invest at depression prices, you need capital."

"But I'm simply selling someone else's machinery for a commission."

"So you see, all that vision is useless without capital. Just think for a moment. Bear with me now. Imagine, instead of selling someone else's machinery for a mere commission, if you *owned* the machinery you were selling. Think of it. Millions. Or better yet, if you owned the company that was making your marvellous machines. Imagine!"

Stanley shut his eyes and imagined. Somewhere beyond the wealth, he thought he glimpsed a vision of the woman he had been dreaming of that very night, Monica James.

"But the capital . . ." began Stanley.

"I may be able to help you with that," Pedersen said, setting the hook. "But let's not talk about it now. Finish our drinks, sleep on it, and we'll resume fresh and alert in the morning."

III

LYING ON HIS BACK BESIDE Monica, Cameron listened to the knock, the shove, the lulling, ceaseless, separate, finite lap of each wave on the black, barnacle-encrusted timbers of the dock at Campbell River.

"I could lie here like this all day," he said.

"No. You'll do exactly what you said you would do. Don't you remember? You're going to go ashore with that boy and ask after his father. I'll go with you if you like."

ON THE *CARDENA*, the quartermasters shared a cabin and, as they were now docked in Campbell River and for the moment had no ship to steer, the two men were passing the time in their bunks.

Passage through Seymour Narrows nearing, Briggs brooded over the notorious piece of water that had claimed so many ships and lives.

Wilson was only too happy to provide details.

"It's a dirty piece of water and you must go through it but you must go through when there is slack water, on account of the strong tide. If you are off a half hour either way, you can't go through until the tide changes."

To Briggs, tide was what happened at the beach. When it went out, you saw sand; when it came in, water lapped gently at the shore.

"The tide in Seymour Narrows, how strong is it?"

"It's been known to reach sixteen knots on the flood."

"Jesus, man. Most ships can't do sixteen knots. Can the *Cardena*?"

"No. The *Cardena*'s maximum speed is sixteen knots, so it would be a standstill, wouldn't it? We'd be at full throttle, both steam engines fired up full, but we wouldn't be moving because we'd be fighting an oncoming flood tide."

The senior quartermaster's description of the Narrows had been a cold recitation of technical fact, but when he resumed speaking it was in halting fragments.

"Terrible place to navigate. Have to run it at slack. A sucking whirlpool. Tell you how it works. Pull the plug and watch the water run out of your bathtub. Farther down it goes, more it whirls round and round. Like a funnel, with all the water pushing and shoving to get into the whirl. That's what happens when it's high tide and the water fills all the channels between Vancouver Island and the mainland.

"A trawler started through and the tide caught it. Some old boys standing on the shore on the Vancouver Island side saw the boat caught in the whirl. Went around faster and faster until it was sucked down clean out of sight. Never saw so much as a draw bucket come floating to the surface. Even the masts went down in that hole. It was just the end for every soul onboard."

"Sweet Jesus, man! Don't tell me this. You're scaring me out of my wits!"

"But you asked. You've been asking me about the Narrows ever since we left Vancouver."

"Yes, but it's me who's got to stand watch and steer through this thing with him."

"Oh, don't you worry about Captain Boyce. He only goes through on the slack. That's how he got his nickname, Slack Jack."

"I thought you said he was called the Fog Wizard."

"Well, that too. They call Jack Boyce a lot of things. Now go wake him because he likes to take his time with his coffee before he takes us through the Narrows."

HE HAD KNOWN Seymour Narrows in all its moods—in the middle of a big ebb, its waters rushing up to Ripple Rock, where they broke, whirling into cauldrons. He remembered one morning, fog in the Narrows so thick he could see neither the bow of his ship nor the deckhand he had posted there as a lookout, and then, out of the blankness, he heard the insistent sharp blasts, five, of a ship in distress. Closer now, the deckhand at the bow saw it first, so close they almost collided: The CNR steamer *Prince Rupert* had passed the *Cardena* farther up the strait and now was stranded on Ripple Rock.

Sooner or later Seymour Narrows will find you, thought Boyce. That particular morning the Narrows had found two ships in the fog: the one, the crippled *Rupert*, carrying a full load of passengers, with its port propeller spinning in mid-air and the starboard one jammed in the rudder, was pinned to Ripple Rock and perilously close to the looming cliffs; the other, the smaller *Cardena*, was attempting to rescue the *Rupert* in the strong ebb tide.

Boyce's first mate, an old-time halibut fisherman with huge hands, heaved a line and the *Cardena's* steel towing line was made fast to the *Rupert's* stern. The towline was taut with tons of pulling force as Boyce stood at the aft telegraph, working the controls in the manner of a tug moving a liner. The *Rupert* wouldn't budge. He rang for Full Ahead, and slowly the big ship scraped across the rocks and floated free. Once the *Cardena* had pulled the *Rupert* into mid-channel and away from the threatening cliffs, Boyce began towing her into Deep Cove, a mile from the Narrows entrance. It was a tough tow, the jammed rudder causing the *Rupert* to swing wildly back and forth. By the time they were out of the Narrows and safely into shelter, the fog had begun to lift, still stubbornly clinging to the shore, hanging in the treetops, obscuring the mountains.

A gangplank was placed between the two ships to transfer the *Rupert's* passengers to the *Cardena*. From the bridge Boyce watched them make their way across to his ship. They were dressed in their finest: tweeds, ties, and caps, the women elegant. You never would have thought that half an hour ago they had been stranded on Ripple Rock, their ship in peril of being flung against the cliffs.

"SKIPPER!" BRIGGS RAPPED loudly on the captain's cabin door. He hated this part of his job, banging on the door and calling out until he got a response that would ensure his captain was awake. "Sir!"

At last Briggs heard some stirring in the cabin and muffled words as if the old man was talking to himself.

BOYCE HAD BEEN dreaming he was in Seymour Narrows again and now that he was awake, he was filled with memories of other voyages and the men he sailed under.

Boyce had sailed for two years as a third and second mate to accumulate the twenty-four months of experience required to write the exams for his master's ticket. Like almost all of the first generation of Union Steamship skippers, Boyce's mentor, Captain Findlayson, had come over from Scotland. A true sailor who got his master's ticket aboard clipper ships sailing around the Horn, he had gone to sea at the age of fourteen on the clipper ship *Glenmorag*. When he was twenty-six he got his master's certificate and went over to steam.

He joined the Union Steamship Company in 1911, and one of his first commands was to take the old *Lonsdale* to Japan for scrap. The ship nearly sank in heavy seas; with water in the bilges, water in the forepeak, and a broken steering chain, somehow they made it to Japan.

When Findlayson got back to BC, he signed on to the *Chelohsin* as third mate. He had a master's ticket and so could sail all over the world, but he had demoted himself to third mate to learn the hazards of the BC coastline.

"Look," he once told Boyce, the two of them studying the charts in the wheelhouse of the *Chelohsin*. "It's one thing to be a deep sea skipper. It's quite another to be a captain on the Inside Passage. This is the most intricate, convoluted coastline in the world."

Findlayson wanted to know every inch of it, and whenever the *Chelohsin* was docked in an inlet or cove, he would launch a lifeboat with a deckhand to row him around so he could take soundings with a leadline, which he then recorded on his charts. When he retired, he passed these annotated charts and logbooks on to Boyce just as Boyce would pass his own charts and logbooks on to Wilson, for Boyce already knew the mate's quartermaster was preparing to write his mate's ticket.

This realization gave Boyce cause to wonder whether the Union boats would always make weekly calls at one hundred and fifty isolated communities, camps, canneries, and settlements up the coast. He sensed hard times ahead. Anyox was struggling over low ore prices and he had heard talk of shutting down the mine completely and cutting back the Union Steamship schedule in the coming winter.

He remembered the upturned, expectant, familiar faces of people on docks. Would they always be there, waiting for the weekly call of a Union steamer? In his memory he heard the sound of a woman at the end of a fog-bound dock banging on the bottom of a pot to guide his ship in while behind her, unseen in the fog, the whole community waited on the dock, trusting he wouldn't take it out.

IN CAMPBELL RIVER, the bar, more correctly called the beer parlour, had signs above separate entrances: MEN'S and LADIES'. "Well," said Cameron, unaccustomed to sitting on the ladies' side, "here we are."

The trio sat at a small round table with an orange terry cloth cover that stank of spilled beer. They were the only patrons on their side of the bar, but the din from the men's side could be heard through the wall. "So it seems," said Monica.

"How old are you, son?" asked the bartender.

"Eighteen," lied Matt.

"That's still underage. I'm afraid I'll have to . . ."

"It's all right," interrupted Cameron. "He's with us."

Cameron's words were spoken to placate the bartender but they had an immediate effect on Matt, Monica, and Cameron himself, and in the silence that followed, each of them pondered their meaning.

"Very well," said the bartender, "but I'm holding you," he glanced at Monica and Cameron, "responsible."

Their beer glasses were filled to a white line painted just below the rim of each glass to ensure patrons were not cheated. A notice pinned to the wall in a hastily executed scrawl announced MEAT DRAW CANCELLED. The bar was a cheerless, gloomy place of small minds and green bitter beer in small glasses filled to the white line, no more, no less.

Cameron thought the chance of encountering loggers on the ladies' side nonexistent, so he proposed to leave Matthew with Monica while he checked out the men's section. No one liked this arrangement but Cameron promised he wouldn't be gone more than a few minutes.

In fact, he was gone for twenty minutes, which seemed to Monica and Matthew an eternity, and when he returned he was accompanied by a man who appeared to come from another world.

He wore Stanfield wool underwear and suspenders that held up his pants, and black rubber gumboots cut off just above the ankle.

"This is Shakey Jake Thorenson," said Cameron. "They call him Shakey Jake because he works a cedar shake claim out of Menzies Bay just north of here. He's logged all his life and he claims he knows your dad, Matt."

Thorenson was a big man but he couldn't stand up straight. A life clambering up side-hills setting choker cable had bent his back to the slope of the hills. Two fingers were missing from his right hand, blunt stubs bitten off back of the knuckle by steel wire choker cable.

Monica instinctively glanced away from him as a thing foreign and abhorrent. Sensing this, he looked at his mangled hands and said, "You may not know me, or like me, ma'am, but men like me have been around since the beginning of time. You can't build a house without lumber, and you can't clear the land without loggers."

He knew all the legends: Roughhouse Pete, Black Angus Macdonald, Spooky Charlie Lundman, and Pegleg Whitey Hoolan. He worked with them in the woods, drank with them on the Union steamships that took them to camp, and when he was on a blow in Vancouver, a city he referred to as "the big smoke," he partied with them in the Balmoral Hotel on Hastings Street, the Occidental on Carrall, and in Tommy Roberts's saloon. And—this was the part Matt found at once both disquieting and reassuring—he knew Matt's father.

"Yes, I know your father."

Matt listened, spellbound, while the man talked on.

"Your father went hand logging with nothing more than a hand saw and a jack. You get a log a day into the water you're having a good day. Your claim has to be overlooking the water, and it has to be steep. The steeper the better. You have to fall each tree so it will slide down the hill as far as possible. If you're lucky, it'll slide all the way into the water."

Jake Thorensen lifted the small glass to his lips and emptied it in a single motion that ended with wiping the foam from his lips with the back of his bad hand.

Matthew saw it was shaking. Cameron ordered another beer for Thorensen. He hadn't touched his own. Thorensen seemed to be reflecting, his eyes on that faraway hillside.

Thorensen drained his glass and stared into its bottom.

Cameron watched Monica, wondering what she made of it all. It had been her idea, after all, and now they had to see it through, but the way Cameron saw it, they were finding out about Jake Thorenson, and very little about Frank Clayton.

"What about my father?" asked Matt. "Where is he? Where is my father?"

Thorenson shrugged. "Back in the bush somewhere. Said he'd try it on his own."

"But I thought you knew where he was," said Matt.

"I said I knew him. I didn't say I knew *where* he was. Thanks for the beer though."

"You can have ours too," said Cameron. "We've got a boat to catch." He pushed his untouched glass across the table.

OUTSIDE THE BAR, the three unlikely friends—a boy who couldn't find his father, a high rigger who moved from logging camp to logging camp, and the mistress of a mine manager—were now making their way along the boardwalk back to their ship.

What, they wondered, had they learned? Cameron wanted to talk about it with Monica, but not with the boy present, for Cameron was beginning to fear the worst. Frank Clayton, it seemed, had willfully turned his back on everyone, even his own son, and simply walked into the woods and disappeared. Or worse, he could be dead.

BOYCE UNROLLED THE chart titled *Discovery Passage* onto the table, weighted down one end with his wooden sextant box and the rolled-out end with his coffee mug, checked his watch, and stalked out of the wheelhouse onto the bridge.

"Damn them!" he cursed from the bridge, searching the wharf for his missing passengers.

Campbell River was a terrible place to dock. Rough water sometimes battered the wharf so that one minute the dock was above the ship's deck, the next minute the ship towered above the dock. Passengers were helped ashore with extra ropes, and crew members carried the children. Sometimes the weather was so bad the ship couldn't dock and they just had to keep right on sailing up the coast.

But today was the kind of day that made poets out of mariners, and poetry out of life on the sea—smooth water, or as smooth as it gets around Campbell River, the jingle of tackle, and masts bobbing in the wake of small craft off-loading freight on a summer day. Passengers leaned over the *Cardena*'s railing to call out to friends, and on the bridge above them Jack Boyce, who should have been exchanging pleasantries and final farewells with the people on the pier, paced and cursed. The mail and cargo had been unloaded, the engine room was on standby, and he had been ready to sail thirty minutes ago but he was missing three passengers.

Where were they, anyway? He had told them, *warned* them, to be back so he could sail in time to make the slack in Seymour Narrows. What angered Boyce most was that he had momentarily lost command of his ship to the whims of three wandering misfits who were not, it now seemed, coming back to the *Cardena* and who had already made him late for the slack tide. He couldn't allow that to happen. He was leaving without them. He might still make the slack if Mackinnon gave him Full Ahead.

CAMERON, MONICA, AND Matt were on the far side of the freight shed when they heard the departing blasts of the *Cardena*'s whistle, and as they came round the corner of the shed they saw their ship leave the dock. Matt jumped onto a horse-drawn freight wagon, climbed to the top of the load, and waved his hands wildly above his head.

"Stop!" he shouted, his voice lost in the distance.

Cameron and Monica ran down the length of the narrow pier.

Onboard the *Cardena* the passengers had all moved to the port side to watch the plight of the stranded trio. Koko leapt from his mistress's lap and raced up and down the deck. Poking his head through the railing, the dog saw Matt on the dock and began to bark furiously.

What was Boyce to do? Leave three passengers stranded on a dock in full view of everyone watching from the *Cardena*?

Besides, he knew the boy's father. No one had seen him in over a year, but Boyce could remember when Frank Clayton had travelled up the coast to his timber claim on the *Cardena*. He couldn't leave the boy behind. He rang the engine room for Full Stop.

"What the hell!" Mackinnon was unable to see what was happening on deck. "Has he lost his mind?" Now he was ringing for Slow Astern. It didn't make any sense.

Boyce manoeuvred the *Cardena* alongside the dock and the gangway was hastily thrown down. There was no time for lines. A cheer went up from their fellow passengers as the delinquent trio scrambled onboard. Koko wouldn't stop barking until Matt was on deck and then snapped at his heels, as if scolding him.

"Fools!" Boyce muttered to himself, for none of them understood the peril they had placed the ship in.

ONCE THE SHIP was safely under way, Mackinnon left the engine room and went above deck into the wheelhouse to see Boyce, curious as to why Boyce had rung Slow Astern.

"It's the boy. Frank Clayton's boy and Cameron and that damn woman. They've made me late for the Narrows."

Boyce had already forgotten why Matt had gone ashore at Campbell River but Mackinnon was well aware of the boy's plight, his dwindling finances and diminishing hope. Matt needed a job and they decided to make him a day man.

"We'll get Grayson to rig out a bosun's chair," said Boyce.

Mackinnon thought he caught a glint of mischief in the old man's eyes.

"The boy can paint the mast. He'll soon stop pining after his father."

If only it were that easy, thought the chief, but the boy's demons were deeper than Boyce's simplistic solution.

The *Cardena* steamed north full ahead out of Campbell River up Discovery Passage toward Seymour Narrows, and it fell to First Mate Allan Grayson to find Matthew and inform him that if he wished, he could be taken on as day man.

"What does the day man do?" asked Matt, looking out the port side as they passed half a dozen smaller craft anchored in Duncan Bay.

"Just about everything," enthused Grayson. "You see, you're a sort of floating relief man who goes where he's needed. The rest of us work twelve hours a day in six-on, six-off shifts but the day man only works an eight-hour day."

"Yes, but what does the day man *do*?"

"Well, you're responsible for keeping the ship tiddly."

"Tiddly? I never heard such a word. Don't you mean 'tidy'?"

"No, I mean tiddly."

"But what does it mean?"

To Grayson the word was so common a part of a seaman's vocabulary he'd never considered its actual meaning. He said, "See that brass bell there above the fo'c'sle hatch? It's all tarnished inside. If you polish that bell until it shines, then it would be tiddly. And the varnish on the mahogany door on the port side of the wheelhouse, it's starting to blister. If you sand it down and paint it, then it will be tiddly. Same thing with that railing there, where the rust is lifting the paint. If you scrape and chip away the rust and wipe it down with kerosene, and then paint it, that's making the ship tiddly. The idea is to make the whole ship tiddly. That's your job."

"That's it?"

Grayson nodded. "Pretty much."

"Sounds like a glorified janitor to me."

"Well it's not. Sometimes," added Grayson, lying but knowing he could make it happen on his own watch, "you get to steer the ship when the quartermaster needs a break. Look, do you want the job or not? I thought, and the crew thought, that you could use the money. Pay's thirty-five dollars a month."

He had tried to make the job sound important, necessary, an integral part of the ship's operation. In fact, it was a fiction created by the entire crew. It was their way of taking care of the boy. Though they hadn't let on to Matt, some of them knew Frank Clayton and feared what might happen to Matt when he found him.

"Well?" asked Grayson impatiently.

Matt nodded.

"Right then. Let's go to the rope locker and break out the bosun's chair. Skipper wants the mast painted."

Grayson began to lay out the bosun's chair, a contraption composed of rope and pulleys by which, Matt was beginning to understand, he must hoist himself up the mast and, after painting it, lower himself down again.

"Couldn't I start at the bottom and work my way up the mast?" he asked Grayson.

"No, course not. You'd smear paint all over yourself and the mast and make a hell of a mess. No. What you've got to do is work your way down from the top of the mast, always reaching up above you with the paint brush. Easiest thing in the world. Nothing to it, really. Just don't look down."

"Don't worry, I won't," Matt said, and shading his eyes from the sun with his hand, he looked straight up almost a hundred feet to the top of the mast, from which there now seemed no escape.

The *Cardena* was passing the rocky bluff that jutted out from the Vancouver Island side of Discovery Passage. Race Point, ahead, Maud Island could be seen to starboard, and on the Vancouver Island side, Menzies Bay.

Since they'd left Campbell River Matt had seen tugs and fishing boats holed up in every little pocket and bay, and now he saw half a dozen boats gathered in the south part of Menzies Bay. "What are all those boats doing?" he asked.

"Waiting for the tide to turn," replied Grayson.

It seemed an innocent enough answer. But Matt knew nothing about the water or how to read it, or that by "tide" Grayson meant tidal stream, which off Race Rock was now in flood, and that in the Narrows, it would reach the maximum speed of which the *Cardena* was capable.

"Looks like the skipper's going through on the flood," said Grayson. "Well," he shaded his eyes and glanced up at the gulls wheeling overhead, "you'll get a bird's eye view of it from up there. Ready?" He began to pull on the rope, hoisting the boy strapped in the chair aloft, the open paint can dangling on a hook from the chair. "Don't spill any paint."

Matt didn't answer.

JACK BOYCE AND the *Cardena* had left Campbell River late, and the tide waits for no one, nor can it be stopped. He had missed the slack and was now facing the full force of the flood in Seymour Narrows—two miles long and less than half a mile wide—the restriction in the body of water between Vancouver Island and Quadra Island. Through this narrow passage rushes the tidal stream. The flood sets south and the ebb north.

"Well, Briggs, we're in a bit of a sticky wicket here," Boyce said to his quartermaster. "But don't you worry. Old Archie Mackinnon will pull us through. In the meantime, keep to the east of those heavy swirls off Race Point. Once you are abeam of it, begin your turn into Seymour Narrows. You must avoid the rips that extend half a mile south of Maud Island. Once we pass the Maud Island light, we will set a course to pass North Bluff on Maud Island at about mid-channel. There's one other thing, Briggs."

"Yessir?"

"At some point this flood tide will stop us in our tracks but even though we are not moving, you must hold the ship steady. We must hold our course in the tidal stream."

ON THE VANCOUVER Island side of the Narrows, a family of picnickers had made their way up from Campbell River to see first-hand the channel of water that had claimed twenty-four ocean-going vessels and over a hundred smaller craft.

They had just spread a blanket, the mother passing sandwiches to the father and two children, when out of the south they saw a ship coming toward them. At first it was just a dot on the horizon, a spume of black smoke rising into a blue sky, but as it came closer its details gradually became more distinct.

By imperceptible degrees, the *Cardena* was slowly losing speed as it ran into the force of the tidal stream. As this force became stronger, the ship's speed diminished until both the crew and passengers noticed it.

"The captain must have rung for a decrease in speed," Karl Pedersen commented to Shanks.

It was a reasonable explanation, yet neither man could recall hearing the telegraph ring.

Archie Mackinnon was above deck, playing cribbage with one of the deckhands in the mess room, when Briggs came in on his coffee break and the chief engineer got wind of what Boyce was up to. He dropped his cards on the table and ran down to the engine room.

"Pour on the fuel," Mackinnon shouted to his fireman. "Boyce is going to take her through and we're bucking a flood tide. Fire this thing up and keep her right up to a full head of steam because I'm going to open her up as far as she can go."

THE FAMILY WAVED from the shore and the passengers on deck waved back but the ship did not pass. The picnickers stood on the rocks and waved and waved, their arms churning the air above their heads. For the passengers onboard the *Cardena*, the continued presence of the family onshore was a constant reminder that the ship was not moving forward and that there was no need to wave, and one by one they dropped their arms despondently.

Word that the *Cardena* was caught and held captive in the tidal stream spread throughout the ship, and anyone who had not been on deck before was now. Passengers leaned out over the main and upper deck railings and stared at the picnickers. Occasionally someone would still raise an arm to wave but then think better of it, for they all now realized that the presence of the picnickers in exactly the same place they had been in half an hour ago was evidence of the tide's supremacy over the ship.

"WE'RE MOVING, AREN'T we?" Stanley Shanks peered over the railing and watched the water stream by the ship's hull. "Aren't we?"

As in a stopped bus or train when the conveyance next to you begins to move, creating the momentary illusion that yours is moving, so too the water that rushed by the *Cardena* created the illusion of movement, but the ship remained stationary, stopped by the strength of the tidal stream.

"'Fraid not, old boy. 'Fraid not."

Shanks looked at Pedersen. "What will happen to us now?"

"Dunno," muttered Pederson. "Dunno. Best thing for it is to just enjoy the day. One thing's sure: I have every confidence in our captain. I have seen him with this very ship, the *Cardena*, pull a much bigger ship off the rocks right here in the Narrows."

"Rocks! There's rocks here in the Narrows?"

"Yes, that's Ripple Rock right over there." He pointed to where the water seethed and eddied around the unseen but deadly outcropping.

"My God," said Shanks. He gripped the railing with both hands and stared at the water whirling around Ripple Rock. "What have I done? I even brought Martha with me!"

"Let me think," began Pedersen in a casual way, as if making idle conversation instead of speaking of past and pending marine disasters. "Yes, it was three years ago, in '27, same month as this too, I believe, August, when Boyce and the *Cardena* pulled the Canadian National liner *Prince Rupert* off that very same rock there, Ripple Rock.

"Not to worry. The man is a master. Pulled the bigger ship off the rocks like the *Cardena* was a tugboat. You look a little green. What say we go to the bar? I'll buy you a drink and tell you how this mining stock could work into your future. Trick is to get in at the beginning."

"No. No. I can't. I don't feel well."

"Good God, man! You can't be seasick. We aren't even moving."

"Just nerves," said Shanks, and thought to himself, that was the whole point: they weren't moving. If he didn't get to Port Hardy on schedule he would be ruined.

He had mailed invitations and posters all over the north end of Vancouver Island—Telegraph Cove, Beaver Cove, even to Sointula and Alert Bay—announcing a demonstration of an amazing invention that would revolutionize the logging industry. If he and his two assistants and their equipment did not arrive in Port Hardy by

Saturday night, Sunday at the latest, he was ruined. Almost all his wife's money was invested in the equipment and the wages of the two Swedes required to operate that equipment.

BELOW DECK, MACKINNON'S precious engines rattled and shook as if some greater power had seized the *Cardena*. Not the crew, not the engineer, nor even the captain now controlled the ship. After entering the inland waters off the north end of Vancouver Island, the tidal stream had moved down Johnstone Strait, bottlenecking in the boiling waters of Seymour Narrows where it met the *Cardena* head on with its full force.

Another skipper would have waited it out in Campbell River, shrugged it off, and simply said, "That's all right. There's plenty more tides in the book." But not Boyce. He was going through against the flood.

"Damn him," Mackinnon cursed. Why, he wondered, is he doing this?

THE FAMILY ON the shore stopped waving and pointed at the mast. The idea that the mighty *Cardena* could be stopped dead by the current was strange enough. But what was a boy doing hanging from a rope halfway up the mast?

FROM HIS POSITION up the mast, Matt could see, ahead of the ship, the course they were to take. It was as if they were going up a river. At its mouth, the river was wide and the force of the stream was dispersed. Farther upstream, he could see the river would narrow and the current pushing against the boat would be stronger.

The most difficult part was not to tip the paint can, which dangled from the bosun's chair on hooks, and not to be scared, which he was. Worse, against Grayson's advice, he couldn't help himself; he looked down. From this dizzying perspective he could see the entire ship from stem to stern.

Midship he made out Emily who, unlike the other passengers, seemed unconcerned over the plight of the *Cardena*, contentedly sketching with Koko at her feet. He looked for Cameron and Monica but didn't see them.

The forward deck was crowded with Chinese cannery workers. They were dressed in overalls, sitting on anything they could find. They had crates of chickens and pigs with them. One of them was wearing a suit and seemed to be in charge. Some of them were smoking clay pipes with long stems.

An Indian family stood apart. The mother wore a wool shawl across her broad shoulders. Her son, a boy about Matthew's age, stood beside her. She held a smaller child by the hand. The mother's black hair was parted down the middle and shone in the sun. How Matt envied them, for he sensed, by the care with which they stood close together, that they were a family. For this reason alone he considered them lucky. Though he could not see the father, he believed he was not far away, just as, in his more optimistic moments, he believed his own father was not far away.

Matt had only to look out from his aerie to see beyond the shoreline into the mountains, scarred and ravaged, it suddenly occurred to him, by men just like his father. He was out there somewhere. Matthew *would* find him. He would find his father if he had to search every inch of the coastline. But he couldn't think of that now, or anything else except painting the mast and not spilling the paint, or his guts, all over the deck.

THE PLIGHT OF the *Cardena* was now the preoccupation of everyone onboard, with the exception of Monica and Cameron, who had only to look at each other to know what the other was thinking, and so, without saying a word, they left the others on deck and made their way to her cabin.

In that small space they were at first very awkward with each other, fumbling, filled with misgivings and inadequacies. They willed themselves to believe they had all the time in the world, though they knew it not to be true. In this way they were able to ignore everything outside themselves. And so they began to explore and finally to know each other.

Afterward they lay in a kind of spent stasis, heightened by the fact they were on a ship, so that he felt he was floating or that at any moment he might levitate. It was as if all consciousness had been obliterated. And yet he had only to turn toward her and they were embracing again, her hands clasped behind his neck, pulling him toward her.

She looked into Cameron's face but the man she saw was not Cameron. With instant and sudden recognition, she realized who Cameron reminded her of. Once, in another life, she had been in love, crazy in love, with Bill Chalmers. They had moved in together and were about to be married but it never happened. Something went wrong. Now, in the arms of another man, it was all coming back to her. Cameron's blue eyes, blond hair, even his slightly awkward gait all reminded her of Bill Chalmers.

Cameron looked into Monica's eyes, watching them slowly, by degree, changing colour, from a deep green to a washed-out pale yellow. "What are you thinking about?" he asked. "I mean, right now, what are you thinking about?"

"Nothing in particular," she lied. "You know, just drifting. I'm back now."

He watched the green returning to her eyes.

THEY DID NOT know how much time had passed, perhaps an hour, perhaps two, and wanting to hoard their time together and not let go, to keep the feel and smell of her on him, he did not wash when they dressed and went back on deck. There they found that the ship was in exactly the same place as before, the picnickers still on the shore. Perhaps time had stopped.

"I wish it would," she said.

"Wish what?"

"Time would stop."

"Maybe it has."

They stood together at the railing, their bodies touching, sensing each other even through their clothes.

ON THE UPPER deck, Martha Shanks sat with a school teacher returning from summer vacation. The two women watched Cameron and Monica on the deck below.

"I cannot," Martha began, "simply *cannot* understand what he sees in that woman. I don't understand the attraction."

"Attraction?" repeated the school teacher. "Hmm. Rather like a magnetic or animal attraction. Very strong. Overwhelmingly so, I suspect. Just what do you think they were doing all last night in her cabin and again today? Something has got a hold on them, you see. An energy. And there is this about it: whatever is happening to them is out of their control. That is the exciting and also frightening part. It is out of control. Anything can happen."

"How do you know this?" asked Martha.

"Oh," replied the school teacher. Her hand encircled Martha's thin wrist. "Believe me, I know."

TWO HOURS HAD elapsed since Matt had been hoisted up the mast, and now he had to piss so hard he thought he might burst. The only solution was to paint as quickly as possible to get down the mast. As soon as he had completed his task and felt his feet securely on the deck, he dashed past the Indian family and the Chinese cannery workers and down the forecastle hatch into steerage, and relieved himself in the first toilet he could find. In his haste he had overturned his paint can, and a pool of black paint had spread across the deck.

When Matt returned, he saw Grayson tapping the lid on the paint can shut with a hammer. He had soaked some rags in kerosene and wiped the paint off the deck. "Feeling better?" he asked.

Matt nodded.

"That's good, but did you happen to notice the sign over the toilet you used down there?"

"No," said Matt. "Why? What does it say?"

"Indian Toilet."

"I don't see what difference it makes when you have to go bad enough."

Grayson looked at the boy as if seeing him for the first time. The *Cardena* was changing Matt. It was as if he had gone up the mast one person and come down another. Matt felt the change the moment his feet hit the deck.

"Flood tide's letting up a little and we'll soon be through," Grayson said.

He didn't mention the spilling of the paint. That's the way the *Cardena* was. If they liked you, they kept you on as crew. If they didn't like you, then you never sailed as crew on their ship again.

Boats were beginning to shoot the gap from the north, struggling to maintain control as the south-flowing tidal stream carried them through.

Emily continued sketching. On the entire trip, this had been her only opportunity to sketch the shore when the ship was not moving.

IV

THE *CARDENA* SURGED AHEAD THROUGH the last of Seymour Narrows and into Johnstone Strait, a narrow, sixty-eight-mile-long channel with mountain ranges rising abruptly from the water's edge.

"I feel as if we are passing through a gate into another world," said Monica.

On the port side of the *Cardena*'s passage, the road that followed the northeastern shore of Vancouver Island had now ended. For the communities beyond Seymour Narrows there was no road access; the *Cardena* was their only link to the outside world.

And on that summer afternoon when the westerly breeze rose at midday to boom down the strait, the very air being drawn down Johnstone Strait seemed to come from another world, where the land and waterways were wilder and lonelier and the last vestiges of society seemed farther and farther away.

All afternoon they moved among small islands, the sun casting a glaze upon the wrinkled surface of the sea. A pod of killer whales passed between the islands with them, black triangular dorsal fins emerging, disappearing, then re-emerging as they rolled tirelessly on.

"They're feeding on the salmon," said Cameron.

Suddenly one would rise and lift its huge mass completely out of the water. Sea water streamed from its slick, black and white, arcing shape as it broke the surface, shook itself loose, and hurtled into the air, the sun catching, for a brief moment, the pure snow white of its belly before its weight carried it crashing down again into the sea.

When the whales surfaced Monica tried to count them. Sometimes she thought there were eight in the group, sometimes it seemed more like ten.

"A family," said Cameron. "A mother and her offspring who stay with her for life."

"YOU CAN SEE our ship's reflection in the water," said Matt.

He was painting the railing midship on the main deck. Behind him, seated with Koko, her sketchbook open, Emily stared straight ahead at the subject of her sketch, a mountainside rising so steeply out of the sea it seemed almost perpendicular, a wall of green forest that rose straight from the very tidemark with cedar, hemlock, spruce, and fir.

Matt stood on the bottom rung of the railing, using it like a ladder to gain the height from which he looked down at the ship mirrored below him, an odd sensation. It was like standing onshore and watching the *Cardena* pass by, but no, he was onboard, on the ship, on deck, looking down at the flagship of the fleet, as it moved through the water.

For the crew, the *Cardena* was more than an inanimate object carrying cargo and passengers. The ship was a living entity, with a personality each member of the crew knew intimately.

The passengers believed that the crew served them but this was not the case. The crew served not even the captain but the ship itself, and of the passengers, only the boy was aware of the ship's personality, for the crew had adopted him, invited him into their world. The *Cardena* was licensed to carry two hundred and fifty passengers and that summer took on more than capacity. The final frontier runs into the ocean and all manner of humanity walked the *Cardena*'s decks: miners, loggers, gamblers, fortune seekers, Indian and Chinese cannery workers.

The crew was used to dealing with all kinds of people but didn't know how to respond to the boy looking for his father or what to tell him. They were accustomed to students travelling alone on the *Cardena* to attend high school in Vancouver, but this boy was different. They watched him wander the ship, as if searching for something or someone, exploring every nook and cranny of it. He opened the hatch on the forward deck and climbed down the metal ladder into the netherworld below deck. He visited the deckhands in their dark, rank quarters. He went into steerage.

"Can you help me?" Sudden, unexpected, and urgent, the boy confronted the crew. "I'm looking for my father. Have you seen him? I've got to find him. I know he travels this same route on the *Cardena* to get to the camps where he works, so you must have seen him. Frank Clayton is his name."

The crew allowed him to explore their ship because for many of them, the *Cardena* was a haven from the failed or flawed lives they had fled on land. And in his newly appointed role as day man, Matt was also a junior member of the crew. To the other passengers, the ship was a mode of transport; for Matt, it was becoming his home, the crew his family, and so they set about, in subtle ways, to make the ship a haven for him too. They placed a stool in a corner of the wheelhouse and another in the engine room behind the chief engineer's control station. Or so it seemed. Perhaps there had always been an extra stool for a visitor in the wheelhouse and one also at the engineer's station, but Matt was made to feel welcome to use them.

MATT LEANED OUT over the railing and stared trance-like into the reflection of the ship in the water below.

"Don't fall in!" Emily called behind him, her voice pulling him out of his reverie.

The mountains were changing, the green forest cut and stripped, the earth bare and brown, as if, thought Emily, some demented monster had gouged a swath out of its side.

"Is that one of the places your father works?" she asked.

"Could be. A logging camp is always moving."

Yes, she thought. Wreaking devastation and then moving on.

"When was the last time you saw your father, Matthew?"

"Almost . . ." He was trying to remember but Emily's question confused and troubled him. In fact, the family hadn't lived together since his father had gone back to logging. Two or three times a year he would journey down to Vancouver to visit but then this too had stopped. "Over a year, anyway."

"And you haven't seen him since?"

"My dad will be waiting to pick me up. The captain has instructions on how to get me to my father. You'll see."

"You don't have to shout, Matthew. People are noticing."

But the truth was, if he saw his father now, he didn't even know if he'd recognize him.

MONICA JAMES WAS a woman of indeterminate age, somewhere on the far side of thirty. She smoked Gitane cigarettes and when she couldn't get them, Gauloises, and when she couldn't get *them*, Gauloises tobacco, which was best of all, for it came in tins and was moist, but then she had to roll her cigarettes and sometimes her hands shook.

She wore a scent that she bought in strange shops under a number of names, Indiscretion, Distraction, and sometimes the simple name that most accurately described it, Musk. As a consequence of both the distinctive and memorable smell of the exotic tobacco in her French cigarettes, and the overpowering fragrance of the musk, her scent lingered wherever she went on the ship. It hung in the air in the bar and hovered over the tables in the dining room, and it was driving Stanley Shanks mad.

It was the custom to invite passengers into the wheelhouse where they could see first-hand the navigation of the ship. The quartermaster stood at the wheel and held the ship steady on course. The captain stood next to him, his hand resting on the ship's telegraph. The polished brass, the sextant, the unrolled charts, the elderly, distinguished captain dressed in his dark navy blue uniform all inspired confidence in the ship and the men who ran it; that confidence had been shaken by the recent fiasco in Seymour Narrows but was now restored as passengers saw from the scene in the wheelhouse that all was proceeding according to the carefully plotted plan of the captain and his crew. They didn't see the scraps of paper he had stuffed into his coat pocket, the forgotten notes written to himself, or that when he stepped out of the wheelhouse, the light of day turned his navy blue captain's coat to a purple faded with age.

IT WAS AFTER one such visit to the wheelhouse by Monica and Cameron that Boyce found himself pacing back and forth in the small space in an agitated manner. Finally, he called for a deckhand to wipe the wheelhouse down with bleach and throw open the windows to drive out the woman's scent.

Boyce turned to the purser and said, "I absolutely forbid that woman to enter the wheelhouse ever again. She'll drive the men to . . ."

"Distraction?" offered the purser, amused by the old man's vulnerability.

"Yes. That's it. We won't be able to keep the ship on course."

"WE'VE GOT TO help Matt find his father."

Ever since Cameron had told Monica about the whale pods, how the families stay together, she had been talking to him about Matthew.

"It must be terrible for him. Here he is, alone on this ship. We should, shouldn't we?"

"Well," Cameron began, stalling, trying to think of something to say, "he must have had someone, somewhere to go after his mother died."

"He was staying at his aunt's. His mother gave him a ticket to Prince Rupert. Told him to go find his father. This, you understand, was when she was dying."

Cameron didn't answer, just stared at her. Why was she so concerned about Matt? All Cameron could think about was the time they had spent together in her cabin. It was as if their love making had never existed or meant nothing to her.

"That kid is all I ever hear about."

"You don't understand, do you? I mean, what he represents." ·

"I guess not."

"He represents potential. What it is still possible to become. Unlike us, a man who kills trees for a living, and me, a worn-out, middle-aged mistress of a mine manager. And even while we sit here talking, Matt's chances, his possibilities, are diminishing."

"I don't see what that's got to do with me and you."

"All you think about is yourself, your appetites, which, as I have discovered, are considerable."

"And what about you, Miss Holiness? What does the boy mean to you?"

"I already told you, possibilities. When I look at him," she paused and stared off into space, and then said, wistful, a little sadly, "when I look at him, I see the mother I might have been."

But Cameron didn't see how he could help.

"I thought you were a logger. That you might have run into the boy's father somewhere."

"I'm a high rigger. I come in just before the crew that does the actual logging."

Cameron had more or less invented his trade as he went about it. Climb a one-hundred-and-eighty-foot-high tree, cut its top off with a double-bladed axe, hang two lead blocks from it, and rig them with steel cable. He didn't know the logging crews and he'd never met Matt's father. He went from camp to camp on the Union boats, performing his dangerous task, then moving on to the next camp.

What he did know was the terrifying moment when he axed

through the crown of the tree and it let go, the severed tip whipping back and forth across the sky, him hanging on for dear life.

In the silence that was growing between them, Cameron and Monica leaned against the railing and watched small islands slide by on the starboard side of the ship.

"Beautiful, aren't they?"

"Beautiful?"

"The trees."

He had never thought of them in that way. He who climbed to the top of the tallest of them, who made the first cut in the felling of entire forests, had not seen their beauty until now. The woman beside him made him see it. He had climbed them, cut off their tops, and now, for the first time, he saw what they were. Yes. They were beautiful.

"There's land for sale on some of these smaller islands," he said. "And I've bought a piece. We could build on it."

"Build? You and I? Build a house? You're mad. Crazy."

"About you, yes. About this, no. This can work, believe me. We can make it work."

Cameron's experience with women was limited. He had never known or dreamed a woman like Monica existed and, having just experienced undreamt-of gratification, was falling hopelessly hard and fast in love.

Monica was shaking her head as though she couldn't believe what she was hearing.

"It's waiting for us. Waiting for you and me, Monica." He was telling her how the coast was rich with food. "Salmon, halibut, cod, clams, crab. You'll never want, Monica. I promise you. Not as long as we're together."

"Stop, Cameron. Please stop. It can't be. Ever. Don't you see? Living in a rainforest makes no sense to me. I'm not from the coast. I've never lived in the country. It wouldn't work."

"We can make it work," he pleaded.

"No, we can't. You're getting off at Port Hardy and I'm going on to Anyox. You have a job to do, and I'm going on to the copper mine. It's not you, it's me. I can't do it. I'm sorry. Truly sorry. I just can't do it."

She looked into his face, saw the depth of his hurt, and tried to mollify him. "Let's not spoil what we have. Let's make the most of the time we have left together. Can't you be satisfied with what we have now?"

"No. No, I can't. It's all or . . ." he started to say "nothing," but caught himself, realizing what a desperate corner he'd backed himself into. "Where are you going?"

"To my cabin. I need some time to myself."

CAMERON NO LONGER knew what would happen to him. His life was suddenly out of control, and as in that wild, panicky, out-of-control moment when the top of the tree let go, all he could do was hang on and hope. He couldn't, wouldn't let go. He hardly noticed where he was as he paced furiously forward and aft, passing his fellow passengers without greeting or acknowledging them.

He must pull himself together. Simply walk off the ship in Port Hardy and go to his job in the woods. He would continue as if nothing had happened, resume life as he had lived it before, but that was the problem—he couldn't.

And what about her? With a woman like that there would always be someone, he thought bitterly. The idea of any other man being with her drove him mad with jealousy. Yet that was where she was going, to the mine manager at Anyox.

A few passengers were sitting about comfortably, their faces smooth and at ease, enjoying the sunlight and the sea air.

Karl Pedersen was playing ping-pong with a tall young girl. It was the perfect game for the fat man, his girth covering his entire end of the table. All he had to do was effortlessly move his arm to perfectly plunk the ball in place, all the while plotting how he would relieve Stanley Shanks of his wife's inheritance.

On the port side, Cameron walked through a game of shuffleboard, almost knocking over the players. As if pushing against a great wind or some strong invisible force, his tall frame bent forward as he strode past Emily and Matthew without even seeing them.

EMILY WAS BUSY, working to sketch the features of the shore from the deck of their moving ship.

"What's happened to Cameron?" asked Matt out loud, as much to Koko who was sitting in his lap as to the artist engrossed in her sketch.

"Loss of sense of self," she muttered, without losing the rhythm of her rapid strokes. "Loss of sense of self."

Through her reading of Whitman, a worn copy of whose work she carried in her bag, and by listening to her friend and mentor, Lawren Harris, she had come to understand this loss of sense of self as part of the artistic process.

"There," she sighed, as if she herself had just returned, and looking up from her book, indicated she was finished.

As Matthew leaned over to pass Koko back to Emily, he stole a glance at her sketch. It didn't look like trees at all but swirling lines of strange energy forces.

Emily quickly closed her sketchbook. It was not meant for the eyes of others.

"Is that a bad thing, Emily, loss of sense of self?"

"Artists experience it all the time, but Cameron is not an artist, and for him it might prove fatal."

Matthew stared at Emily's sketchbook cover, titled *Ontario Blank Drawing Book*. The publisher, W.J. Gage & Co., had decorated it with an innocuous border of maple leaves.

On Emily's lap, Koko, ever alert, stared straight ahead, guardian of some secret knowledge.

FORE AND AFT, port and starboard, Cameron paced the length of the *Cardena*, a man contained in a place he no longer wanted to be yet could not escape from. Though they were apart, Monica's scent and the feel of her body were still on him and that too was torture, for he was aware their time together was drawing to a close. Still, she couldn't stay locked forever in her cabin and so he paced the ship, waiting for her.

He rounded the forward deck and at last there she was, her back to him at the railing, her hair blowing in the wind.

He rushed forward.

"Monica, I . . ." His hand was on her shoulder.

Startled, the woman turned to face him and he saw it wasn't Monica at all.

"I'm so sorry," he muttered.

MONICA ALMOST REGRETTED what she had done, but no, she wasn't sorry. She had wanted a one-night affair and she had seduced Cameron, wanted him from the moment she first laid eyes on him on the dock in Vancouver, but she had, it seemed, got more than she bargained for. Cameron was in love. Damn him anyway. Didn't he know the best time was now, when their passion was at its peak? That if they were married, living together, their love would slowly diminish until it became lost in the inevitable rhythm of everyday life?

If only she could talk to him, say, look Cameron, we are middle-aged adults. Don't you think it's a little late for us? But she couldn't talk to him that way, couldn't even bear to see the hurt in his face, so she had locked herself in her cabin.

He just couldn't accept the fact that when they reached Port Hardy they must part, she staying onboard the *Cardena*, he going to his appointed job in the woods. High rigging, whatever that was.

Well, it was over. It had to be. How could it be otherwise? Somewhere, deep down inside her, was the truth she was trying to avoid. That she had fallen in love with him and she was afraid of that love. It didn't fit her plans. One had to have a plan: hers was Stuart Jenkins, the mine manager waiting for her at the Anyox copper mine. But did she have a contingency plan? Jenkins had paid for her ticket, and if someone told him about her affair with Cameron onboard the *Cardena*, she might as well stay onboard and go back to Vancouver. What had started as a one-night fling was turning into something so serious it frightened her and the only way she could deal with it was rejection. Here was the thing, the deep thing she was most afraid of in a relationship: she had to maintain control, and with Cameron, she had no control. This was terrifying.

She had told the boy Matthew it was important to have a contingency plan. Very well. What was hers? To remain a kept woman? To turn her back on something she didn't even know was still possible, the love of a good man? Because that was what was most endearing about Cameron—that he wanted her not for a night or for his amusement, but to be his partner for a lifetime.

"I want us to grow old together." Those were the words that stayed with her, that she could not forget. What would it be like, she wondered, staring out the porthole of her cabin, to live with Cameron, to grow old together?

Unanswering, the land slid silently by as the *Cardena* made her way up Johnstone Strait, the trees sombre, shrouded in mist, the rainforest she knew nothing about, where Cameron seemed so sure they could build a life together.

She closed her eyes and from somewhere within the ship heard strains of music, fragments of a familiar melody repeated over and over. The band had set up in the lounge, going over and over a difficult passage. The song they were rehearsing was "My Heart Stood Still." They couldn't get the bridge right.

V

"HELLO, HELLO!" IN THE WHEELHOUSE Boyce was talking into the radio phone. "This is the *Cardena* calling with ETA for Kelsey Bay, approximately thirty minutes from now."

The ship passed Helmcken Island on her port side, a low land mass set in the middle of Johnstone Strait that acted as a natural obstacle dividing eastbound traffic from westbound, then Hardwicke Island, fifteen miles long with the summit of Mount Royston at its centre, its main village on the western side of the island opposite Kelsey Bay.

Monica and Cameron stood together on the far forward main deck of the *Cardena*. They had reconciled themselves to the fact they would be parting when Cameron left in Port Hardy. They had little more than a day left together and were trying to pretend it was just like any other day. Both of them were doing their best to put on a brave face, but there was no cure for it; the lovers were running out of time.

If you had come upon them from behind as they leaned over the rail and looked intently down into the water below, you might have thought they were both about to leap overboard, but in fact, because of where they were standing, they were looking at something they alone could see.

Below them, two porpoises were criss-crossing ahead of the sharp wedge of the ship's steel bow at a speed only slightly more than the

Cardena's, so that they avoided a collision by moving always just in front of the ship.

Were they trying to communicate with the ship? Did they sense the presence of Monica and Cameron above them? Their sleek forms shot forward.

In the wheelhouse, Boyce blew the ship's whistle and the deckhands bent over the heavy, coiled lines on the main deck. The ship was coming about for a starboard landing at Kelsey Bay, a small indentation on the west entrance to Salmon Bay at the mouth of the Salmon River. In the engine room, Mackinnon readied himself for Boyce's telegraph signals to manoeuvre the ship into the dock. Both the deck crew and Mackinnon knew it would be a starboard landing because of the strong current off Salmon River.

"I'M GOING TO walk up the pier," Cameron said to Monica when the ship had docked. "Come with me."

"No," she said. "I think I'll stay onboard." Already she was distancing herself, steeling herself for the time when they would be apart.

They avoided each other's eyes by looking back down into the water, but the porpoises were gone and instead, under the bow, the couple saw the hazardous rocks of the bottom.

From the bridge, Boyce looked down into the water swirling around the pilings. He had to bring the bow of his ship right in over a rock and if he came in too fast, he would hit it. They couldn't have built the wharf in a worse place, but he had docked there many times and always, it seemed, the same girl, like a beacon, stood at the end of the dock, looking up at him. There she was now.

The whole village converged on the landing, walking singly and in groups on the pier that juts on pilings out into Kelsey Bay. Standing at the end of that small dock, I watched the *Cardena* come closer, for it was a beautiful thing to see, Captain Boyce and the *Cardena*.

It is an act of faith to stand on a tiny dock while a two-thousand-ton ship slowly bears down on you, and I once saw a navigator who knew no better try to make a port landing with the *Capilano* in Kelsey Bay. More than one dock has been sliced in half by a Union boat.

But that day you could tell Captain Boyce was on the bridge by the way the ship was handled. It was like watching a waltz: forward, backward, slide, one, two, three. Captain Boyce docked the *Cardena* as if she were his dancing partner, and perhaps she was, for there was not a single scuff or scrape of timber or piling, the ship coming to a complete stop inches from the wharf it never touched.

A deckhand heaved a line from the ship to our wharf and someone slipped its spliced loop-end over an iron bollard. The telegraph rang for Slow Ahead, and when the bow and stern lines were made secure we all breathed a sigh of relief. The moment when everything could go horribly wrong had passed, and as the lines were made fast, we applauded.

As if in acknowledgment, Captain Boyce appeared on the bridge, placed one hand in the pocket of his double-breasted coat and the other on the bridge railing, and looked down at us standing on the dock, or so we thought, all of us looking up at him. Perhaps Captain Boyce only looked down to check the lines, his eyes hidden in the shadow of the peak of his hat, but I believed he was looking at me and I dreamed of dancing with him on the afterdeck of the *Cardena* that fall when I went to Vancouver to go to school.

A pallet of freight was emerging out of the ship's hold. The winch man swung the pallet out above us and we looked up to see the deckhand standing on top of the freight, his upraised hand clenching the rope, the daring young man on the flying trapeze. He rode the load down to the dock, the crowd parting, stepping back to make a space where he and the pallet would land, and then we rushed forward to claim our freight.

A woman suddenly burst from among us with a parcel pressed to her chest. Gulls shrieked and swooped above the wharf. It was all there. New valves for Father's steam donkey, yeast for Mother's bread, Carnation milk, thread, grease, boom chains, saw files, yards of cloth, cake from Woodward's, salt, butter, and serge pants. The purser had candy bars to sell, and fruit and newspapers not more than a few days old. The good ship that brought us good things.

Clutching bags, packs, parcels, and suitcases, passengers felt their way down the cleated gangway. There was a boy, not one of the passengers getting off, who got off with them for the hour's unloading. You couldn't miss him, he stood out so. He seemed very lost, out of place, as if not a single soul in the world knew or cared about him.

He was going up and down the dock asking for Frank Clayton. Said he was his son, which was certainly news to me and everyone else. Did we know him? Where could he be found?

Yes, we did know him. But where he was now? No, we didn't know and good riddance to the man. Somewhere up the coast was all we could come up with. A lot of people knew Frank Clayton, and a lot of people didn't want the boy to find him.

CAMERON WALKED QUICKLY up the pier, the *Cardena* tied to one side of the dock, eight fishing boats and the government telegraph boat tied on the other. He saw Matt asking after his father but didn't invite the boy to join him. There was little more than an hour before the *Cardena* would depart, and Matt had been warned not to make the same mistake as in Campbell River.

Cameron felt good to be off the *Cardena*. Monica had so confused and frustrated him that he had half a mind not to get back onboard. He had been promised a job in Port Hardy, though timber prices had dropped so severely he now seriously doubted that prospect. In the meantime, the thing to do was stay active, keep walking, and not think of the woman. He hadn't yet faced the fact that his obsession made it impossible for him to make rational, objective decisions. A part of him wanted to be back on the boat with her, a part of him didn't. Damn her anyway. Well, he had only himself to blame.

He didn't know how far up the Salmon River valley he walked or that he was talking out loud to himself or that he was not alone. Driven by blind instinct, the need to reproduce in the same river they had been born in, the first of the salmon species, a run of pinks, was returning upriver to spawn, dorsal fins cutting the surface, quivering forms steadying themselves against the current.

Cameron came around a bend in the river and stopped to get his bearings; mud flats on his right became a meadow where he thought he saw a deer grazing, its legs hidden in the tall grass. It was a goat, ginger brown in colour, and beyond, on higher ground, there was a large house that he now walked toward.

The house had a hand-split cedar shake roof and two dormer windows. Longer split-cedar barn shakes sheathed its sides, overlapping like feathers, the cedar weathered a silver grey so that the house, perched as it was on poles, looked like some giant, long-legged bird. On its porch sat an old man.

"Pull up a chair," he said to Cameron.

In the afternoon heat, Cameron had the surreal, momentary but distinct impression that the old fellow had been sitting on his porch waiting for him.

"I don't have long," Cameron said. "I have to catch the *Cardena*."

"I'll drive you back. I've got some freight to pick up on the dock."

Cameron tried to guess his age. He might be eighty, he thought. The man looked as though he had done a great deal of physical labour. Despite his age he had a glint in his blue-grey eyes, as if he possessed some secret knowledge or a joke that only he knew.

"Well," said Cameron, for the sake of conversation, "how're you making out in this depression, old timer?"

"Don't mean anything round here except strangers showing up at our door who don't know how to do much. Esther gives them something to eat. I show them how to fish and hunt. Some stay, some move on. Thought you were just another one of them when you walked in here just now. No, the real worry here isn't the depression, it's the floods."

"Floods?" He'd never heard of such a thing in this country.

"That's why I built this house up on poles like this, on account of the floods. Hastings Mill came in here in 1905 and clearcut the whole valley. Stripped it clean. Now there's no forest growth to slow the spring melt off the mountains so it just pours down in a rampage that tears out the banks of the river, floods fields, and washes out bridges."

"Still," said Cameron, "you seem to have done all right."

"Land sold cheap once it was logged, so I got this place at a good price. They left most of the cedar lying on the ground because there was no market for it. Know what the Indians call cedar?"

Cameron shook his head.

"They build their houses and canoes from cedar. Make clothing from the bark, baskets, their lodges, carved masks and totems. It's a wood so versatile and miraculous they call it Long Life Maker. The planks split along the grain, no saw blade ever cuts into a single wood cell, and each cell in the plank is intact, enclosed. This is the secret of the long life of a hand-split cedar plank—the natural preservatives, the toxic oils are sealed within each cell of the wood.

"And the fools who logged this valley left the cedar lying on the ground. Cream the best, and leave the rest. That's the way this coast is logged. Left the cedar lying on the ground to rot. 'Cept it doesn't. The oils in cedar are such a strong preservative that a hundred years from now the cedar will still be lying on the ground, sound and solid. Built this whole house out of it. C'mon. I'll show you."

Cameron followed him through his house, a marvel of invention and ingenuity. He noticed a wood stove made out of an oil drum plumbed with iron pipe for hot water. Cedar was everywhere, framing doorways and windows, on the walls, wood that was a pale rose in colour, the sapwood a light beige, and heartwood darker. The smell of cedar filled the house with a citrus-like scent not unlike the oils released when pressing a thumbnail into the skin of an orange.

"They call it western red cedar but look how it varies in colour. This is my favourite." His hand caressed a door frame, deep chocolate brown in colour.

They stepped through the back door and out behind the house, where a high fence woven from branches enclosed a large garden. A woman in a long, loose cotton dress was gingerly plucking boysenberries from a bush and placing the ripe, deep red fruit into a bowl.

"This is her world," he said. "She loves her garden."

The woman reached over the fence with the bowl, offering the berries to Cameron. Like her husband, she had an aura about her. It was as if, through a great deal of work and struggle, they had come to be at peace with themselves, with each other, and with their environment. The old man pointed toward a small shed about the size of an outhouse. "My smokehouse," he said and opened the door.

Fillets of pink salmon hung on wire. He had cut the fish so that the two fillets remained joined at the tail and could be hung over the wire. He was smoking the salmon with alder.

"You'd think you'd want to use wet alder for more smoke."

Cameron nodded.

"But no, the secret is to use dry wood and to smoke the fish on a dry day."

He removed one of the fillets from the wire, wrapped it in newspaper, and handed it to Cameron. "Try this," he said. "There's nothing like it."

They walked beyond the garden into the second-growth hemlock now flourishing behind the house. A logger like Cameron would simply crash thoughtlessly on through, but ahead of him the old man had dropped to his knees and it seemed to Cameron that he was kneeling on the forest floor with an almost worshipful reverence.

Bright yellow-orange buttons burst from the emerald green moss, the first of the season's chanterelle mushrooms. The old man picked a handful, then another, and handed them to Cameron. "Take these and the smoked salmon back with you to the *Cardena*. They'll know what to do with them in the galley."

He thrust his hand into a hump in the moss and peeled back the covering to reveal a perfectly preserved old-growth cedar log. "I built my whole house out of cedar lying on the ground like this. It's like hunting for buried treasure." His eyes sparkled. "I have no money but I'm rich. If you plan to catch the *Cardena* today, we should leave now."

Cameron thought he heard a hint of sadness in the old man's voice and an indirect invitation to stay on. "Yes," Cameron said, "I suppose you're right."

The old man had inspired Cameron and for the moment he had forgotten about Monica. Cameron had the land and the old man had shown him what it was possible to do on the land. But this man had something Cameron did not have, a life partner. Without that, Cameron knew, he had nothing.

That evening on the *Cardena*, Matt, Cameron, Monica, and Emily enjoyed a meal of smoked salmon and chanterelle mushrooms in a cream sauce prepared by the galley chef.

They ate in silence, and the meal had a kind of finality, for they all knew that after Port Hardy they would no longer be together. Though he could not stop thinking about the old man and his wife, Cameron did not mention his visit with them to the others: the couple represented the life he and Monica might have shared but that she had already rejected.

This meal, he thought to himself with some bitterness, is the closest she will ever come to that life, and she doesn't even know it. But now that Cameron had purchased a parcel of land, he was more determined than ever to build a life on it.

MATT BROODED OVER an unsuccessful day on the dock asking after his father. Would he ever see him again? At dusk he watched the small islands in the strait form dark clumps outlined against the last light on the horizon: tufts of trees that never moved, locked in the stillness of the sheltered evening sea.

When he finished his duties as day man, Matt spent his evening hours in the wheelhouse. He had no mother or father to tuck him in, to say goodnight to him, so he spent his final waking hours in the security and warmth of the wheelhouse. There, in the semi-darkness, their figures silhouetted in the light that glimmered from the compass, the boy, the quartermaster, and the captain shared the enclosed intimacy of that small space. From this vantage point the captain looked down on the main foredeck, to the bow and beyond into the darkness through which the ship was moving.

Sometimes there was conversation, sometimes there was not. Out of respect for the captain, Matt and Briggs seldom spoke unless they were spoken to, although Boyce sometimes shared with Matt and the new quartermaster a story about some landmark as they were passing it. Just as often there was silence, and in that silence, as the ship made its way through the dark waters of Johnstone Strait, Matt sat on the stool in the wheelhouse and puzzled over the strange circumstances he found himself in.

Since he had talked with Emily earlier in the day he had been trying to recall the last time he and his father had spent time together. It was on Vancouver Island, before the move to Vancouver that ended everything.

Parksville was a small village with a few loggers, long two-man handsaws propped against the sides of their shacks, and fishermen. Even now, in the wheelhouse, if he closed his eyes, Matt could hear again the sound of each incoming wave mingle with the voices of fishermen returning across the dark water of the bay. In the evening he ran along the beach to meet the boats and stand behind the men who crouched at the edge of the shore, gutting their catch.

He remembered his first fishing trip—Matt was eight years old— he and his father skidding the small wooden boat down to the edge of the water, carefully sliding it over pieces of beachwood so they wouldn't scrape its painted bottom. He remembered it all, how when they put the lure in the water, a 4½ Tom Mack 50/50 spoon trailing behind a Gibbs herring dodger, they checked its action; the spoon had to zigzag behind the herring dodger, not roll. While his father rowed, Matt paid out the line, counting the strokes between the reel and the first eye on the rod.

Strike! Line screaming from the reel and at its end, its twisting form shaking into the air as it tried to dislodge the hook, the salmon plummeted back into the water with a smack.

After they netted it, the huge salmon lay between Matt and his father, the thwack and pump of its tail beating out the last of its life in the bottom of their boat. Each time his father bent forward to pull on the oars, Matt could see the pride in his face. Father and son in an open boat, rowing into Northwest Bay on Vancouver Island. That was what he wanted: to be again in an open boat with his father.

MEN. THEY MADE Monica tired, wore her down. What she wanted was security, an older man she could humour and control like Stuart Jenkins, the mine manager. In the meantime she had to get clear of Cameron. For now, she would avoid him by staying in her cabin and reading her novel, *Wild Geese*. Once the ship reached Port Hardy, he'd be gone, out of her life.

THE *CARDENA* MOVED inexorably forward toward Port Hardy and nothing Cameron could do would stop it. His life had no direction, or if it did, he did not control it.

SOON EMILY WOULD be off this ship, rid of these people, and her real journey would begin, her last trip up the coast. This time she would travel in a small boat around the tip of Vancouver Island to the west coast and then into a narrow passage no wider than a river. Finally, for her, a woman who had been to Paris and London, and exhibited her paintings in Ottawa, she would be at the very heart, the physical centre of the island she loved and called home.

VI

THE CONSTANT CLACKCLACKCLACK OF PLAYING cards shuffled by expert hands, conversation, laughter, the clink of glasses, and floating above the blue haze of cigarette, cigar, and pipe smoke, the sound of someone playing the piano.

Stanley Shanks and his wife entered the bar just as a gaunt man dressed in black reached across the table to rake in his winnings. The gambler looked up from the crumpled bills and coins he was collecting to size up Stanley, and decided not to try to engage him while he was with his wife.

The gambler and his partner worked in concert to cheat the other two players at the table. They never went on deck, or took the air. For them, the ship's only function was that it provided a table for card playing and, most importantly, passengers to fleece. They made money going up the coast and coming down, and at the mining camps they relieved the miners of their wages. They had a whole bag of tricks they employed, according to the level of sophistication they sensed in their adversaries.

The card sharks were merciless and took so much money from their fellow passengers that when the two men slept, in the early hours of the morning, they barricaded the door against robbers and kept a revolver on the table.

THE PIANO PLAYER, who might have been eighty, was something of a mystery. No one knew where he came from. No one saw him during the day. He never appeared on deck. Perhaps he was simply too infirm and so stayed in his cabin during the day, but which cabin? Was he an employee of the company or a passenger? No one knew.

A persistent but unlikely rumour was that the piano player was the captain himself. Though this was possible, as he only played a one-hour set, it seemed unlikely.

A more plausible explanation might have been that he was a friend of Boyce's whom the captain contrived to have onboard for each voyage, for it was known that Captain Boyce was a great lover of music. Yet if this was so, why did Boyce never appear, even momentarily, in the bar when the man was playing?

Each night at nine thirty the same attractive young woman would help the elderly man to the piano where he suddenly came to life, his whole being bent over the keys.

There were those in the bar who paid no attention to the piano player and his music, the gamblers, for instance, and Karl Pedersen, the portly stock promoter intent on his own designs. But the piano player had gathered about him a small regular audience. Even the *Cardena*'s band, the Musical Mariners, couldn't stay away.

He was playing in the style of Earl Hines, impishly tossing off complex confections with hands as fast and light as those of Phineas Newborn Junior. Just beyond the keys at the far right of the piano, he kept a glass of brandy that he occasionally sipped, glancing over the crowded bar to gauge the effect of his playing. He did not sing, nor was his playing like a concert; it was intimate, as if you were being invited into the private world of his piano playing.

"THAT WOMAN IS a tramp. I'll say it again. T-R-A-M-P spells tramp."

Stanley had to admit Monica did have a certain way of walking that was quite wonderful. Quite unlike anything he had ever seen.

"But surely, my dear, it's none of our . . ."

"Yes, it is, Stanley. It most certainly is. She's even got that boy under her spell. I have it on good authority this isn't the first time she's wreaked havoc on the *Cardena*. She's a predator. I'm sure she knows that the boy's father is an influential and successful logging contractor. That's why she's attached herself to him. And just look how she's carrying on with those men at that table right in front of us. She's as much a predator as those eagles you see in the trees waiting to swoop down on the salmon as they enter the river to spawn."

In his mind Stanley had become the salmon, and the woman, the eagle. Now she was spreading her wings . . .

"Yes. Oh, yes!"

"What's that, Stanley?"

. . . enfolding him.

"Yes, dear. I *do* see what you mean."

"Oh, Stanley. I'm so glad for once we agree."

IN THE BAR, strangers fell into the easy familiarity of fellow passengers who knew they would be together only for a brief voyage. Though they might not admit it, even to themselves, each man was sitting at that table because of the woman.

Since she had come out of her cabin late in the afternoon, Monica had been drinking. She did not feel uncomfortable being seated at a table with six men; she was used to being at the centre of things. Incidents occurred around her: a shooting in San Francisco, a stabbing in a bar in Seattle. Yet she emerged from each fresh disaster unscathed. A true innocent. Or was she? She would look right at someone with those wide green-as-glacier-water eyes and the person would know only one thing, that she was beautiful. Always she had kept moving, an unstoppable force, and like a glacier she left rubble in her wake. One thing she was sure of, her beauty. The men sitting at that table couldn't keep their eyes off her, though some tried.

The heavy scent of her perfume hung in the air. Musk. Some men could take it or leave it. Others it drove mad. It was a little like the Gitane cigarettes she was smoking. If you didn't like them you were all right. But if you did like them, and you never forgot the taste of that dark tobacco, well then, you were hooked.

She sucked on the end of her cigarette till her cheeks caved in and the tip was glowing red.

"I'm from California," she announced, removing the cigarette from her lips and exhaling. "Going to the Anyox copper mine to see the manager there. Do you know him?" She paused and plucked a fleck of tobacco from the tip of her pink tongue. When no one answered her, she said, "Stuart Jenkins is his name. In the meantime," she continued, "here we all are." It was a fact no one could deny.

But the only man who mattered to her was nowhere to be found. She couldn't very well search the ship for him so she kept on drinking.

The smoke hung in the air over the heads of the half-dozen men who sat around her. They were entranced and they didn't even know her name.

EVERY WEEK BOYCE navigated this dangerous coastline, but who could safely navigate or account for the uncharted and shifting currents between a man and a woman?

, He had thought he and his wife would always be together, that at the end of each voyage she would be waiting when he came home, but now the house he came home to was empty. She had died suddenly while he was at sea. Nothing is fixed forever.

It was almost midnight. Matt had already left the wheelhouse for his bunk and Boyce stood over the ship's telegraph, staring out into the night, trying to get his bearings and clear his thoughts. The boy's mother was dead, no one seemed to know where the father was, and Matt was onboard his ship.

First Mate Grayson stood behind Boyce with a mug of coffee in his hand, ready to relieve his captain at midnight. The mate had come into the wheelhouse early to discuss the dilemma of the boy. The third man in the wheelhouse, the new quartermaster, Briggs, stood behind the brass wheel, his outstretched arms moving it back and forth so the compass points rolled equally on either side of the median as he listened to the conversation between the captain and his first mate.

"We can't take the *Cardena* into every unknown little hole just because we think the boy's father might be there."

"That's true," acknowledged Grayson. "And we can't keep up this charade of day man's job forever. He was scared to death up that forward mast. What do you propose to do now, send him up the aft mast? Suppose there's an accident. After all, he's our responsibility while he's on this ship."

"You handle it then. You're better at this sort of thing than me."

The steadfastness of his ship was all Boyce knew now, not this constant flux and change.

But before Grayson took over, Boyce produced a small notebook from his right jacket pocket and carefully printed in neat block letters THE BOY on a page that he then tore from the notebook and placed in his left pocket. His pockets were stuffed with scraps of paper intended to jog his failing memory. Later, when he removed and read one—a reminder of a navigation hazard, a special freight pickup, a message for someone up the coast—he would wonder over its lost and forgotten meaning.

CHIEF ENGINEER ARCHIE MACKINNON considered the *Cardena* his ship and when he described it, he did so with an attention to minute detail he knew none could equal or question, focusing always on how the components of the ship worked. He came by this honestly enough. He had written the exams. He had his steam tickets.

If, God forbid, some malfunction occurred and a repair was required, often precipitated by a navigational error by the captain, if anything on the ship was damaged, he and his men would have to make the repair. The deck crew, the captain and his officers, the passengers, all were counting on the engineer to keep the ship running, and he had been running the *Cardena* since it left the ways seven years before on its initial voyage out from Scotland. Still, like a jewel he kept turning in his hands, the *Cardena* was always revealing some new facet of herself to him. Yesterday in Seymour Narrows he had opened her twin triple-expansion engines to their maximum and they had not let him down. Yes. He loved the *Cardena*, which was why, though it was past midnight, he found himself pacing back and forth in his tiny cabin, holding a copy of the company's standing orders in his hands.

His accommodations were not nearly as commodious as the captain's: a thirty-inch berth fitted with a spring mattress and drawers below, a writing table with drawers, a settee locker covered in leather, a wardrobe with a shelf and four hooks, wash basin, mirror, and toilet rack, folding chairs, an enamelled iron rolled-rim bath. Even though his cabin was not as generously appointed as the old man's, the chief believed he was the captain's equal or superior. It was he, the chief, who kept the ship running, who controlled the power, the engines, who knew how it all worked.

But the captain? Mackinnon did not understand how his mind worked. What was Boyce thinking, stranding them in the most hazardous stretch of water on the coast, Seymour Narrows, for more than an hour, engines full bore ahead but going nowhere, fighting a full flood tidal stream? He couldn't understand why Boyce had subjected his, Mackinnon's, precious engines to hours of stress, never mind putting the ship and everyone on it in peril.

If they missed the tide there was always another one. It was simply a matter of laying over and waiting for it. It wasn't as if the Union boats were expected to keep to schedule. They got there when they got there. Simple as that. What was Boyce trying to prove? Mackinnon had his own copy of the company's standing orders and he intended to confront Boyce with it.

Masters and officers must distinctly understand that
the safe navigation of the ship is to be, in all instances,

their first consideration. They must run no risk, which, by any possibility, might result in an accident. They must always bear in mind that the safety of life and property entrusted to their care is the ruling principle by which they must be governed in the navigation of their ship, and no saving of time on their voyage is to be sought at the risk of accident.

Item 18, *Standing Orders of the Union Steamship Company of British Columbia Limited.*

To make matters worse, to add to the insanity of fighting the tidal stream in Seymour Narrows, Boyce had the band play on the afterdeck and a piano player in the bar. Every time Mackinnon heard the band, to his ears it sounded worse. They played a new music called jazz.

VII

THE *CARDENA* EASED ALONGSIDE THE BC Packers wharf, its bow pointed in at the community of Alert Bay on Cormorant Island. As soon as the ship docked, winches began pulling pallets out of the hold and lowering them onto the cannery dock: food, hardware, all the supplies needed for an isolated community accessible by sea alone.

The salmon season was in full swing, and at the dock a seiner was unloading into holding bins. Inside the cannery, conveyor belts carried the fish to a machine that gutted and trimmed them. In the humid heat of the cannery, Indian women packed cans with salmon. The winch man would load pallets of canned salmon stacked on the dock into the *Cardena*'s hold for the return trip to Vancouver.

It would be a quick unloading, then loading, a little over an hour, hardly enough time to go ashore, but Matt had decided to go anyway. Cameron was content to stay near the docks and pass the time talking to the fishermen.

KARL PEDERSEN, MARTHA SHANKS, and Monica stood on the main deck looking in at the village. Monica couldn't bear the garrulous Pedersen or for that matter Martha Shanks and regretted not going with Cameron, but then, she realized, he hadn't asked her.

"What is that lovely new building in the distance?" asked Martha, pointing through the steam billowing from the cannery's smokestacks. The rancid odour of fish was pervasive, and a constant flow of fish guts spewed out of the cannery into the bay.

At the end of the curving shoreline, a massive, three-storey, red-brick building exuded an institutional sterility that seemed oddly out of place in Alert Bay but that Martha, herself terribly out of place, found reassuring.

"That, madam," said Pedersen, "is the new Saint Michael's Indian Residential School building, a joint undertaking of the Anglican Church and the Department of Indian Affairs. It opened just last year."

"How perfectly lovely," chimed Martha.

Monica thought it an ugly eyesore.

"Has its own farm, cattle herd, garden, water, and electric lighting plant," added Pedersen, warming to the subject. "Accommodates two hundred boys and girls from seven to fifteen years of age brought here from all along the coast. Truly an ambitious social experiment on the grandest scale. Why, they say it cost two hundred and fifty thousand dollars to build. Imagine, in this economic depression."

"It does seem a little excessive," admitted Martha.

"The white man's burden," intoned the corpulent stock promoter. "It is our Christian duty to civilize these people."

Why, Monica wondered, can't these people be left alone? Why are we always interfering? What makes us think we're better than they are? She looked to the right of the residential school at the houses skirting the shore. Women were laying salmon on branch frames to dry. She watched Matt make his way along the boardwalk.

THE MILLWRIGHT FROM the cannery came aboard to visit the chief engineer and brought a bottle with him. He passed it to Mackinnon who opened the porthole, took the cap from the bottle, threw it outside, and said, "This stuff won't keep, you know."

The rank smell of the cannery drifted into the chief's room. Mackinnon tilted the bottle, took a gulping swig, passed it to his friend, and moved to close the porthole. "Know what that stink reminds me of?"

"No, I don't," replied the millwright, knowing he wouldn't get out of Mackinnon's room until the bottle was empty and the tale told. "Bet it smells like a story, though."

"This happened on the old *Coquitlam*. They brought her over in sections from Glasgow and assembled her in Vancouver in 1892. Then they rebuilt her for the Alaskan run in 1897. Her hull was iron, not steel. That's why she's lasted so long. A real workhorse, the *Coquitlam*. Now there's a name for you. Know what it means?"

The millwright shook his head.

"A small red salmon. So there we are, coming across Queen Charlotte Sound in a ship named after a small red salmon when, what do you think, she loses her wheel. Prop falls off, no propulsion, no way of contacting anyone, the ship just drifting out there in the open sea."

"There's nothing much worse, more helpless, than being adrift," said his friend.

"Anyhow, the *Venture* came along on its way north and towed us back to Alert Bay, exactly where we're tied up, here at the cannery. They sent a propeller up from Vancouver but the keyway wasn't big enough. It hadn't been cut as big as the key we had, so we had to file the keyway out. It was quite a job. Hauled the propeller up with chain blocks and tried her on, but we didn't get her right. So we had to take the propeller off and file the keyway a bit more so we could get it to fit. You know how they throw all the heads and fish guts in the drink? Well, there I was, you see, yours truly in a bathing suit, wading around in all that slop, fish heads floating around me while I filed the keyway a bit more so we could get it to fit."

"Awful, an awful feeling." The bottle had turned the millwright philosophical. "There's a lot of people like that."

"Like what?" asked Mackinnon, thinking of the fish heads.

"Drifting, like your ship was. No purpose. No direction."

"We see a lot of that on the boats in these bad times," said Mackinnon. "There's a kid on our boat right now with no family, nothing. Doesn't even know where he's going. Just drifting. We gave him a job. Day man. But it didn't help. Hell, he's not even on the ship right now. He's wandering around on the dock. Says he's looking for his father, Frank Clayton. Well, what if he finds him? Maybe he won't like what he finds. What then?"

"Best thing," said the millwright, "is for a person to find their own direction."

"One thing's sure, it's not a good feeling. When we were adrift in Queen Charlotte Sound my wife was having our first baby in Vancouver and there I was, helpless, not knowing how or when I was going to make it home."

"But you did it, Mac. You filed out the keyway. You put the prop on. It's a great talent, making things run. Fixing things. People don't see it, they don't appreciate it, but it's the basis of everything. Without it, we'd just be . . ."

"Drifting."

They both laughed, a little drunk. It had been a good visit, but Mackinnon couldn't stop worrying about the boy.

That was something he seemed unable to fix.

MATT HAD NEVER seen anything quite like Alert Bay. It had a character, an air about it that he could neither describe nor ascribe to anything he knew. Even before he stepped off the ship he sensed the uniqueness of the place.

Alert Bay was a major service centre off the northern end of Vancouver Island, with the residential school, its entrance flanked by two huge thunderbird totems, a box factory, Cook's wharf, the BC Packers wharf, oil docks, a hospital, a post office, a hotel, and three stores.

With everyone travelling the single road that curved along its shore, and especially now with the *Cardena* docked at the cannery and every manner of conveyance pressed into action along its shore-line road, Alert Bay was a bustle of activity.

The cannery where the *Cardena* was docked sat midway along Alert Bay's shoreline. At one end of the bay was the residential school and to Matt's right, at the far eastern end of the bay, was the Nimpkish Hotel. The hotel had originally been built on the foreshore of the Indian reserve opposite the Indian Agent's office, but five years ago the owners had loaded it on a scow and towed it to the eastern end of the island so they could legally operate a beer parlour.

Matt stood on the boardwalk, trying to decide which way to turn, left or right. After the trouble at Campbell River, he decided he wouldn't go to the hotel, not alone, anyway, so he turned left and before he realized, he was on the Indian reserve.

Now he was in a world that was truly foreign to him, and yet he knew that it was not foreign; it was the heritage and culture of a people who had lived here long before his own. He'd seen totem poles in Stanley Park. They stood just beyond the zoo, a curiosity gawked at by passersby, a tourist attraction. But here, here was where they belonged. Here the poles were an organic part of people's lives.

On the boardwalk two girls were walking toward him. It was the only pathway along the shore so they would pass beside each other. Lonely and not used to girls of his age, he had never felt more confused. What was he to do? Turn tail and run back to the ship? No. He would keep walking toward them, and they toward him, and then the moment would come when they would pass each other. He continued on the boardwalk with purpose and resolve, as if he had an actual destination on the reserve toward which he was walking.

Which, of course, he hadn't. He was an interloper, a trespasser on their land, and his awareness of this contributed to his unease. Whatever plan concocted by missionaries, Indian Agents, and entrepreneurs had induced the Namgish to move from their traditional village site on the Nimpkish River to Alert Bay, whatever else had happened or been imposed on these people, here on this small island, they, not he, were the majority. He was an alien in a place he had no business to be in.

The moment came when they were passing each other. He would not look away. The two girls seemed to gaze directly into him with dark brown eyes, broad full faces, and a confidence he found intimidating.

Eventually he would have to turn and might have to walk by them again in order to get back to the ship. The ship! He didn't know how long he had been walking; he had lost track of time.

Matt was running back now. At the dock they were letting go of the lines. My God. The ship would leave without him. He would be stranded on the boardwalk on an Indian reserve. His boots echoed on the boards and behind him, as he hurried past, he heard the laughter of the girls. "What's your hurry?" they seemed to say.

NO ONE NOTICED the elderly, heavy-set woman and her dog who got off the *Cardena* that afternoon, but she was no stranger to Alert Bay. It had been eighteen years since she had painted *Indian War Canoe, Alert Bay, 1912*—the carved painted dugout in the foreground, the curve of the beach, the community houses in the background.

The residential school, cannery, police station, post office, and beer parlour toward which traffic seemed to shuttle constantly along the road, they were all new to Emily. Instead of canoes, the bay was filled with cannery-owned seiners crewed by Indians unloading their catch. The totem poles she had painted in bright primary colours were weathered grey and almost unrecognizable. But then, who would recognize her as the woman who had stepped off the *Venture* years ago? She looked in vain for the big house she had painted then, two wings outspread across the entire front of the community house, its great protruding beak opening to admit the people entering. It had been replaced by small, soulless white reserve houses.

Emily came back onboard with her sketchbook open, the water-colours still drying on the paper. Everything was changing, and so was she. The poles she had once painted from the front, taking care to capture the detailed work of the carver, she now painted in silhouette from behind, showing the perspective of the beings carved in the poles and imbuing them with a kind of implied life. The viewer of the painting would see as the beings carved in the poles see, looking out upon Alert Bay.

The ship was leaving. Cameron came onboard. Matt barely made it. Monica drew Cameron aside and said, "Promise you'll never again leave me alone with these people."

"Sorry," he said. "Just wanted to talk to the fishermen on the dock."

Still, it was good to hear her say this. Of course, it would have been better if she'd simply said, "Promise you'll never leave me." But no, they'd agreed to separate in Port Hardy and, like a beggar picking up what crumbs he could, he said, "We've got one more stop before Port Hardy and that's Sointula. We'll go ashore together."

"Oh yes, let's," she said, hooking her arm in his.

AS THE *CARDENA* surged back from the dock Emily watched the front of the poles she had just painted recede in the distance. She touched the paper on her sketchbook, the paint dry now.

"Goodbye, Alert Bay," she said to herself, and closed her sketchbook. It was a place she had known from another time, when she was another woman.

Soon she would disembark to travel to the village she had never been to, Quatsino, at the head of Quatsino Sound. What would she find there and how would she see it?

VIII

THE LAST AND MOST NORTHERLY settlement on Vancouver Island, and the departure point for vessels planning to cross Queen Charlotte Sound or go around Cape Scott to the west coast of Vancouver Island, Port Hardy had a final and desperate air about it.

On that late August Saturday, Cameron and Monica were both aware that sometime Sunday they would be parting. Emily too would be leaving the *Cardena* and would be picked up on the return trip south. To Matt, already alone, the breakup of the four friends meant the end of everything.

FROM THE HEIGHT of the deck of the *Cardena*, Stanley Shanks stared down the dock past the men standing around the tin freight shed and considered his prospects. The village, where tomorrow he and his men would demonstrate their amazing machine, was feeling the first throes of the depression. The men on the dock thrust their hands in their pockets and stared up at Stanley on the *Cardena*, looking for something, anything.

What, Stanley wondered, have I done? In the entire village there were only one hundred and forty-two people. What had he been thinking? Still, people kept arriving on the small-craft dock from surrounding settlements as far away as Telegraph Cove. There would be a dance tonight. He dared to hope. All he needed was one sale to cover his expenses; two would be a miracle.

THE NEW COMMUNITY hall in Port Hardy had been built with lumber from a dismantled fish cannery in Shushartie Bay. The doors opened at eight and the band was scheduled to begin playing at nine but it was nine thirty before they took to the stage.

Cameron did not know how to dance but, like everyone in the village, he and Monica were drawn to the hall.

"We can listen to the music," he said.

"I'll teach you," she said, and drew him to her. "Just let yourself go."

But he couldn't. He kept thinking he would step on her toes, for he and Monica were locked in an embrace, pressed cheek to cheek, and she was whispering in his ear.

"Thank you for walking with me in Sointula. I'll never forget that."

"What did you like best about it?"

"When we walked along the road you could look right through the boat sheds, and the whole bay was bathed in afternoon light from the west, and those small Finn houses with gardens and saunas and firewood neatly stacked and drying, so much pride. And something else, a kind of spirit that will always be there. I'd like to go back some day but with you, because that was the part I liked best. I was with you."

She felt his body freeze and realized too late what she had said only made things worse, for tomorrow they would be parting. Foolish, she thought, my foolish heart, and the music, and the night.

IN THE LAPEL of his captain's coat, Boyce wore a white carnation picked from his box garden back of the wheelhouse. You never knew who would want a turn on the dance floor with the captain of the *Cardena*.

It was the end of the first leg of the voyage. Tomorrow it was the open water of Queen Charlotte Sound and up Grenville Channel to the canneries on the Skeena and Nass Rivers and then on to the copper mine at Anyox. In the meantime, he and his chief engineer were having a drink and listening to the band.

"My boys! I'm so proud of them. All my life I've listened to music. Can't do without it. Man's great gift. Without it, well, even though I'm not a musician, I've found a way to contribute in my own way to the band. I get them here and I get them here on time, don't you see?"

And for the first time, Mackinnon *did* see. Amazing, he thought: all that first-class seamanship, in tight spots, risk taking, everything he put me through bucking the tide in the Narrows. It wasn't to haul freight, provide a service to isolated communities, the lifeline of the coast they call us, no! It all had to do with a dance in Port Hardy and getting his band here on time. The old man's lost his marbles. Growing flowers back of the wheelhouse and going on about his band. Damn him anyway.

"Tell you what, Jack. We'll make her into a day tripper and call her a lady, like all the Union's excursion ships—the *Lady Alexandra*, the *Lady Cynthia*, the *Lady Cecilia*—and when your *Lady Cardena* docks on Bowen Island that bloody band of yours can play in the dance pavilion. But one thing you can be sure of, I won't be running her for you. I love the *Cardena* too much to see her turned into a party boat. It wasn't what she was built for and I won't run her for you."

"You're an old grouch, Mac. The only place you belong is down in the engine room. Soon as you get above deck you turn sour."

"And you?" asked the chief. "It's like I told that kid Matt. You belong on deck, squiring ladies around, teaching them how to play shuffleboard."

"Can't stand to see people enjoying themselves, can you, Mac?"

But both men knew they could never leave the *Cardena*. They were inextricably bound together.

SUNDAY MORNING, IN a field surrounded by forest, a crowd consisting of the curious, the bored, and the genuinely interested was gathering at the edge of town. Cameron, Monica, and Matthew had come to the demonstration together. Emily took advantage of the absence of everyone to sit on deck with the whole ship to herself.

The two Swedes, followed by Stanley Shanks, carried the crates across the field and set them down at the edge of the forest. Einar and Ollie undid the crates and began assembling the machine, while Stanley, the forest behind him, turned to address the crowd. They were an unruly lot and he had to shout through a megaphone to be heard.

Monica wandered aimlessly at the edge, tired of watching Einar and Ollie, whose boorish behaviour she had witnessed in the *Cardena*'s bar and who were now attempting to assemble something with wrenches.

Matt walked among the men, asking after his father but with no success. Some wouldn't even acknowledge the boy, preoccupied as they were with the demonstration.

"What's he saying? What's it mean?" They craned their necks to see the little man and hear the phrases and words coming from his megaphone.

Cameron stood at the very front. He had guessed at the impor-
tance of the machine they were assembling, and didn't want to miss
a thing.

"What you are about to witness will change forever the way logging is done on the coast."

"Look at that little pissant in a suit, shooting off his mouth,"
grumbled one of the men. "What does he know about logging? Still,
if what he promises is true it would be . . ."

"Say goodbye to springboards and the crosscut saw."

"Listen. What's he saying?"

He had their attention now. It would be . . .

"A miracle! A miracle of modern engineering! Ladies and gentlemen, I give you the 1928 Stihl Model B two-man chainsaw."

The Swedes had now assembled a motor to which was attached a
thin steel bar; around it ran a chain of razor-sharp teeth.

"No. This is not an electric saw. No cables or power plant to drag
into the woods. The completely self-contained two-man Stihl Model
B chainsaw is powered by its own internal combustion engine."

It was a device that required care, tuning, and being alert to its
idiosyncrasies: a cumbersome thing weighing over a hundred pounds
and, including the single cylinder engine attached at one end, six feet
in length. Einar and Ollie Gunderson had become its masters.

Einar bent over the motor, pulled the starter cord, squeezed and
pumped the throttle, and the saw roared to life. The brothers looked
at each other across the steel teeth speeding to a blur. Every move they
made now had to be done in unison, so that they moved as one, the
saw running between them. This sense of balance and coordination
was difficult to achieve because the saw itself was not balanced, the

weight concentrated at Einar's end, to which the engine was attached. Ollie held the handle at the lighter end.

Moving in locked step, the saw roaring between them, they carried it to the chosen tree. The slightest slip, a stumble caused by loss of footing on the rough ground, could bring disaster of the most horrible kind.

The crowd was silenced by the deafening roar of the saw and the knowledge that at any moment things might go terribly wrong. The wind was up and there was an edgy incipient sense of violence in the air. Someone or something was going to get killed. It might be a man, it might be a tree.

Chips of wet white spruce flew from the cut, the scent of the tree's sap filling the air in a shower of sawdust. They were working on the side facing the field, cutting a wedge-shaped notch that would determine the direction of the tree's fall, cutting halfway into the diameter of the tree.

Einar and Ollie completed the cut and carefully backed the blade out of the tree. They set the idling saw down on some blocks of wood, axed out the last of the notch, and then placed the wedge down on the ground. Cameron could smell the fresh-cut heart of the base of the tree.

They bent to pick up the saw and begin the back cut but while they had been axing out the last of the notch, the saw, running on idle unattended, had stalled. No matter, they thought, Einar pulling back slightly on the starter cord till he felt it was right—if you got it wrong it would misfire and tear your arm off—and straightening up, yanked hard on the cord. But the motor did not fire. This time, he said to himself. I'll throw my whole back behind it, and he did.

A wraith of foul-smelling blue smoke rose from the dead engine.

"Internal combustion engine, eh?" hooted someone. "More like the *infernal* combustion engine!"

Stanley stepped forward into a huddled conference with the two Swedes. "What do you mean, you can't get it started? You fools!" he shouted. "You idiots! That's exactly what I pay you for, and you've let me down. I'm ruined."

"Shut your mouth, you little shit. We run dis show now. Flooded is all. Wait five minutes and she start and we fall your goddamn tree, and if you want we fall every tree on this whole mountainside. Leave mechanics to us. Flooded is all. We wait. She starts."

In this unscheduled pause, a whispered thought began to enter the minds of some of the onlookers. The gigantic tree, with its under-cut halfway through the trunk, was still standing but moving. They looked up at its top, teetering in the wind, the whole tree swaying back and forth. The still-to-be-executed back cut was only a final formality that would bring the tree down, but the tree could in fact topple and crash down at any moment.

The crowd was becoming uneasy. People were starting to drift away.

"No, wait. Please," pleaded Stanley. "In matters mechanical, patience is indeed a virtue. My associates and worthy colleagues assure me we have nothing more than a flooded carburetor, which time alone, even as I speak, is correcting. Ah, I think they're ready now."

Einar nodded to Stanley, adjusted the choke, just midway this time for they must not flood it again, and pulled the starter cord. The saw roared to life, Einar working the throttle as the two men carried it to the rear of the tree to begin the back cut.

FROM THE *CARDENA*, where Emily sat, the roar of the chainsaw was reduced to a drone, like a mosquito. Then the sound stopped and she saw a hundred-and-fifty-foot giant tree slant out of the sky; she covered her ears just in time to muffle the sound of its crash to the earth.

It bounced when it hit the ground, the impact felt underfoot by everyone in the crowd, and as it bounced the tree did a kind of half turn and then settled on its branches with a final rustle.

Emily had spent a lifetime developing a relationship with trees. For years, she had referred to the freshly cut stumps of fallen trees as screamers. Now, as she removed her hands from her ears, she thought she heard screams at the edge of the forest. But it was just the jubilant yells and shouts of the crowd now rushing forward to examine the stump of the tree.

The lifeblood of the tree, its sap—the colour and opacity of amber—welled up from the roots and, with nowhere left to go, pooled on the base of the stump. Seeping to the outer edge, the sap ran with the viscosity of warm honey down the bark and into the earth.

Cameron stood in stunned shock. He counted the time it had taken the two men to fall the tree. Minutes, fifteen maybe, at the most. In his mind he saw the act of falling the tree repeated over and over, clean, quick, and complete, the effect so profound it caused him to have a vision: an entire mountainside clear cut, nothing left but smashed dead waste wood, sawn-off branches, and upturned roots. The iron tread of machines ground the splintered wood into the torn-up earth and bulldozed the slash into massive, separate piles. Men set fire to them and, from each of these piles of smouldering wood, smoke rose, spires of wet wood smoke rising from a whole mountainside, a smoking, barren, burnt wasteland.

When he came to, he found himself staring at the sap pooling and running over the edge of the stump.

"That's it for me," muttered Cameron. "I'm finished."

"What's the matter?" asked his friend, Ricky Gaines, whom Cameron had logged with. "You lose your nerve? That's it, isn't it? You've lost your nerve."

"Maybe," he said, remembering the man in Kelsey Bay who had told him about the clear cut that flooded the Salmon River. "I just can't do it anymore."

His friend accepted this and they spent the afternoon drinking from his bottle and talking over old times.

"The big thing," Gaines said, "we're both alive. Think of that. All those close calls and we're still here. We're still alive! If you're not going to go logging, what will you do?"

"I've just bought a piece of land. I'll see it on the return trip so I'll stay onboard until I get to it." Cameron didn't say where the land was and he didn't mention Monica James.

"Sounds like a plan."

The two friends touched their glasses.

But Cameron didn't have a plan.

IX

"ANY LUCK, MATT?" ASKED MONICA.

"Nothing. The worst part was, and this happened twice, I said, 'I'm looking for my father.' And they just looked at me and said, 'Wattsa matter, kid? You lost?'"

"They didn't mean anything by it. Maybe they thought you *were* lost, that you'd got separated from your father."

"That's a laugh," he said. "I got separated from my father the day he left to go logging up the coast."

It was the first time he had confronted this hard truth. He could say it now, but it only deepened his sense of abandonment and rejection.

They watched Emily stop at the ramp that led to the lower dock for small craft, set her bag down, and turn to wave at them where they stood on the forward deck of the *Cardena*.

Monica and Matt waved back. "What a strange lady," said Monica.

"I like her," said Matt. "I met her on the dock in Vancouver before we boarded the ship."

He was remembering what she had told him about being alone. He watched her make her way down the dock, the sun dropping in the west behind the trees, the *Cardena* backing away from the wharf, and he saw that she was truly alone.

"Hey Matt!" yelled a voice behind him. "Give us a hand with these lines!" On a Sunday evening, Matt's day man duties didn't apply but the deckhands weren't going to let him talk to a pretty woman while they worked.

Bill "Soogie" Phelps bent over the head line, his shirt sleeves rolled up, his tattoos showing. Matt knew all the deckhands now, their names, their nicknames.

"Tell your friend to stay out of the bight!" chimed in Paddy "Springline" McLean. He had been gassed in the First World War, had come over on the *Cardena* from Scotland, and never got off the ship, living onboard. The *Cardena* was his home; the crew, his family.

"Got it!" Matt grabbed a line. He would never be alone as long as he stayed on the *Cardena*.

MONICA TURNED AND walked away from the men working the lines. She was about to step inside, midship, when she saw a man with his back to her standing at the stern. She knew who he was before he turned around.

"I thought I'd never see you again. I couldn't find you in the crowd. We didn't even say goodbye. What happened?"

"I met a friend. We had a drink. Talked over old times. As to what happened, I don't know. When the tree fell, something snapped. Cracked. Splintered."

"Yes," she said. "Everyone heard it."

"No. Something inside me. I can't explain it. When that tree fell, it was as if it fell on me."

"I'm glad it didn't," said Monica, amused, but not understanding.

"Everything changed. I can't go back to logging, and I can't leave you."

"And here you are," she said, flattered, pleased, but knowing Cameron meant trouble. He didn't fit into her plans.

"Yes," he said, astonished. "Here I am." For the first time in his life he felt free. On the return trip he would see his land.

He had thought his life ordered, routine, but being with Monica and then witnessing the chainsaw falling of the tree had changed all that. He no longer knew what would happen and had gambled everything on a split-second decision by getting back on the boat. He saw there was good and bad in Monica, that she could go either way. He could see it in her eyes, the way they would change from deep green to a pale yellow. She had a good side, her concern and care for Matt and himself, and a bad side, wanting to be the kept woman of a mine manager. Could he win her to his side?

The wind was up and no one else was on deck. Monica and Cameron watched the last protection at the northern tip of Vancouver Island recede in the distance as the *Cardena* cut into Queen Charlotte Sound, forty miles of open sea.

They stood at the stern of the ship, holding each other. He looked into her eyes, watching them shift colour, trying to read them.

SEATED WITH MARTHA and Pedersen, Stanley sulked over his dinner, the chef's traditional Sunday offering of roast beef. Not a single sale. Not even a serious inquiry. He had gambled everything and lost. By the time he paid wages to those two churlish louts, he wouldn't be broke, he would be seriously in debt.

Stanley stabbed at his Yorkshire pudding with a fork and then, giving up all pretence of eating, dropped it in disgust into a pool of gravy in the middle of his plate and glowered at it as if it was his mortal enemy. The demonstration of the chainsaw was seen as a freak novelty, not to be taken seriously. He was, as his wife had told Pedersen at the beginning of the voyage, a man ahead of his time.

"You really should try the Yorkshire pudding," urged Pedersen. "Light as a feather. I am told the secret is to not refrigerate the eggs, to make sure they are at room temperature when beaten."

"Yes," muttered Stanley, staring into his ruin. "Beaten. Whipped."

"Is everything satisfactory?" hovered the steward, seeing Stanley's untouched plate.

"Most salubrious," rejoined Pedersen, the steward's appearance suddenly inspiring him to attempt to brighten the gloom with some impromptu humour and, turning to Martha, he said, "Perhaps you have noticed the stewards always carry a small pickle fork in the breast pockets of their tunics."

"Indeed, I have" said Martha. "They use the pickle fork to dish out those small pats of butter onto the passengers' bread-and-butter plates."

"You are very observant, madam. Very observant. If you look closely at the stewards, you will also see a short length of string hanging loose from the flies in their pants."

"I am not in the habit of looking at men's flies, Mr. Pedersen."

"Of course not. Forgive me. But I once noticed the string hanging from the steward's fly and inquired what it was for. The steward replied, 'During mealtimes we are all terribly busy, and if perchance we have to go to the bathroom, all we have to do is lower our flies by pulling on the string, and we are all set. In this manner there is no need to touch our parts, so it is not necessary to even wash our hands afterwards."

"I thought about this and then said, 'That is quite ingenious, but tell me, how do you replace your parts back inside your pants?'"

"'Oh, quite simply,' responded the steward. 'We use the pickle fork!'"

"You, sir," gasped Martha, "are a low and vulgar man, and whether it is you, your story, or the weather our ship is now encountering that is making me ill, I must leave this table at once."

BOYCE AND HIS first mate stood on the upper bridge, coats on, collars turned up.

"It's a dirty night." Salt spray snuffed out the cigarette stuck between Grayson's lips.

"Yes," replied Boyce. He couldn't help wondering whether the Carr woman had made it safely around Cape Scott. Since 1908, first with Boyce on the *Venture*, she had been sailing up the coast on the Union steamships to paint Native poles. Then for a time she stopped coming. Now, here she was again, older but still painting, still searching. What vision, he wondered, would compel an elderly woman to travel alone in a small boat out into the open sea off Cape Scott on a night like this?

"A dirty night and a dusty night." Grayson chewed on his soggy cigarette, threw the butt away in disgust, and spat out some tobacco. "Dusty."

It was a peculiar term, considering there was water everywhere. The bow of the *Cardena* dipped into the big waves, plunging under, then shot up, the sea flooding the decks. Dust, they called it, the fine spray the wind whipped off the peaks of those waves.

Halfway across the Queen's Pond, as Queen Charlotte Sound was sometimes jokingly called, Boyce remembered Captain Findlayson and the night of the worst crossing he had ever made.

Night, halfway across, past that invisible point at which it was better to go on than to turn around, the weather so bad they could do neither, in the middle of nowhere, Findlayson dropped both anchors, and for twelve hours they peered out into a howling snowstorm, seas breaking over the bow, flooding through the bulwarks, ice in the rigging and on the decks. When the storm lifted, Findlayson poured Boyce a tumbler full of scotch.

At least it's not snowing tonight, thought Boyce, looking up at the clouds passing over a half-moon, thinking of Emily.

EMILY HAD TO wait until the beer parlour closed for the mail boat that would take her around the tip of Vancouver Island and into Quatsino Sound. The boat was a twenty-four-foot, Wallace-built, round-bottom double-ender powered by a single-cylinder, nine-horsepower engine built by two religious brothers in Vancouver. The Easthope brothers quoted the New Testament in their catalogue, and their classified ad in *The Vancouver Sun* under "Boats and Engines" proclaimed

Jesus
The Light of the World
See the New Easthope Engines

Emily was already onboard when, sometime after midnight, the two men who would take the mail boat out of Port Hardy stumbled down the dock, unwrapped the *Ida B*'s lines, and lurched onboard, swearing loudly. The engine would not start and the men shouted and cursed, their voices carrying across the water while the boat drifted aimlessly and Emily prayed silently.

Jesus
The Light of the World

Finally, the Easthope single cylinder fired and gasped and wheezed, and pushed the *Ida B*'s white, wooden-plank hull through the sheltered harbour water . . . chukachukachuka.

They were leaving just after midnight to make the high water slack at Cape Scott in the morning and avoid the sea that could break over the Nahwitti Bar. Daylight found the mail boat coming around the cape on the slack tide, but even so waves broke at their peaks into white caps banging into the hull.

Standing legs apart on the rolling deck, the pilot clutched the wheel and searched for the landmark that would tell him to change course, a string of ragged grey rocks breaking out of the ocean's foam on their port side. Suddenly, he turned the wheel and they were in an inlet.

"Slithering," Emily wrote, "through the still waters of Quatsino Sound."

From the deck she could have thrown a stone into the towering cedars and spruce that crowded down to the water's edge on either shore. Around each bend in the channel she expected the village to appear, but there were only the moist, glistening rocks, the gnarled, twisted roots of the cedars, the dampness of the rainforest dripping slowly into the channel. The elderly woman in oilskins sat on two mailbags, her back to a barrel, her dog in her arms. No one spoke to her or asked where she was going. And if they had, what would she have answered? That she was going into the absolute centre of something but of what she did not know and must continue until she found it?

Unwinding eddies slid by the *Ida B*. Emily lay on her back on the mailbags and stared straight up at the shaft of sky cut through the forest by the channel, wondering idly at the lives in the letters that poked at her through the canvas sacks.

X

THAT NIGHT THE *CARDENA* SAFELY completed her crossing of Queen Charlotte Sound. The purser came into the wheelhouse to review with Boyce the stops they would be making in Smith Inlet and Rivers Inlet during the coming day.

"I've got a manifest here for three boom chains for Frank Clayton in Security Bay."

"So?"

"The boy's father."

Boyce's left hand scrabbled vaguely in a jacket pocket stuffed with forgotten memories.

"Frank Clayton's boy."

As soon as the purser left the wheelhouse Boyce reached under the chart table for some papers and began filling them out, all the while giving orders to his quartermaster.

"We'll pass midway between Round Rock and Halliday Island. We must stay clear of the foul ground on the north side of the island, and then steer a mid-channel course through Blackney Channel."

"Yes, sir." Briggs assumed that Boyce, behind him at the chart table, was plotting their course. In fact, he was filling out Matt's discharge papers, and when he completed them, which took only minutes, as the boy had only been with them a few days, he slipped two ten dollar bills inside, folded the papers closed, put them in an envelope, and sealed it.

"Wake the boy," Boyce said to his first mate, Grayson. Both Grayson and Mackinnon had come into the wheelhouse to assist with the landing. "I cannot afford to waste time over a few rusty boom chains."

"No. Wait. You can't do this." It was Mackinnon. "It is past midnight and the boy's asleep, and I say let's just drop the boom chains on Clayton's raft and be on our way and the boy will never know and we'll have done him a favour."

"How so?" asked Boyce. "I don't see it that way at all, not at all. How is going right on by the boy's father, without waking the boy, doing him or anyone else a favour?"

In the semi-darkness of the ship's wheelhouse, Mackinnon was watching the outline of his captain's face: hard, resolute, the face of a man who fought Seymour Narrows to stay on schedule. If he was going to convince his captain, he would have to do it now. If he didn't, or couldn't, then Boyce's view, as senior officer, would prevail, and Matt would be, as Mackinnon saw it, abandoned to a fate worse than . . . abandoned by the whole crew, including himself and Boyce. He said, "Maybe you don't know any of this, and maybe you do. Most of the crew knows and plenty of people up and down the coast know."

"Spit it out, Mac. What are you trying to tell me?"

"Seems Frank Clayton's been leading sort of a double life up here in the woods with Native women. Well, to make a long story short, one of them followed him to Vancouver. Made quite a scene all the way down and when she got to Vancouver she knocked on the door of his house, his good wife answers, and it was all over for Frank Clayton. Demanded he get out and never come back, ever, not even to see Matt. But the boy, he doesn't know any of this about his father. So he's in for a hell of a surprise. Unless, as I say, we just slide on by and do Matt a big favour."

"Maybe. May be the best thing for the boy. But it's wrong, Mac. Don't you see? It's wrong. The boy wants this. Well, we can give it to him and if it turns sour, so be it. But just suppose now, mind, just suppose he gets on with his old man. What then? If you don't give him the chance to find out for himself, he never will. Another thing Mac. You're making moral judgments. Deciding what's right and what's wrong. That's not our job. Our job is to deliver freight and people, and that's what we have here. Some boom chains and a boy who wants to be with his father." Boyce turned to Grayson and repeated, "Go wake the boy."

ASLEEP IN HIS bunk, Matt felt at first as if he was in rough weather, but no, someone was trying to shake him awake.

"Wake up, Matt!" It was Grayson.

Matt began to get up, hastily pulling on his clothes. There must be an emergency and they want all hands on deck, he thought.

"Hurry!" urged Grayson. "Get your gear together. Your old man's out there on a log raft. What a surprise he'll get!"

"Huh?"

"Skipper wanted to give you this." Grayson handed him an envelope.

"What's this?"

"Your discharge papers."

121

"Discharge papers?"

"Yes. You're getting off the ship."

"Right now?"

"Yes. Let's go. Hurry!"

THE SHIP'S TELEGRAPH rang; the *Cardena*'s motion slowed; a spotlight beam pierced the solid darkness, moved slightly, and came to rest on a tiny log raft. In the circle of light stood a bearded logger, shielding his eyes from the glare of the spotlight with his upraised arm, his dinghy tied to the raft.

They were off-loading the boom chains out the *Cardena*'s side cargo doors, which were higher than the logger's little raft, so a ramp had to be set in place, slanting down to the raft below.

Matt stood in the open cargo door.

"You there!" yelled the logger. "Give us a hand with these boom chains, will you?"

Matt was still so dazed all he could do was comply.

"Sure." He picked up the big ring at one end of a heavy chain and began dragging it down the ramp.

When he got the boom chain onto the raft he stopped and studied the man who stood there. Was this the man who would return from his stint in the woods and knock on his mother's door, wearing slacks and a Harris tweed sport jacket—his shirt collar always neatly worn outside the jacket—and present her with flowers?

"Well, don't just stand there. Help me get these boom chains into the boat."

The man on the raft wore Stanfield underwear and pants he had cut off above his caulk boots. But behind the unruly, unkempt appearance, and the full beard that made him look like a wild bush man, Matt saw remnants of his father.

"What the hell you looking at?"

"You don't know who I am, do you?" asked Matt.

"No. Should I?"

"Yes. You should. I'm your son."

"Up here in the middle of nowhere? I don't believe it. Let's have a look."

Squinting into Matt's face, Frank Clayton seemed to be trying to focus or peer through some forgotten doorway that had suddenly and unexpectedly opened.

"Yes, by God! It's you all right. I thought I'd never see you again in this life but here you are. It's a miracle!"

The *Cardena*'s spotlight was suddenly gone and the boy and his father sat in darkness across from each other in the cramped space of a twelve-foot clinker, Matt on the stern plank seat, his father on the middle seat, oars in hand, three boom chains in the bottom of the boat between them.

Matt watched the *Cardena*, outlined by its lights, ease back from the log raft into the night.

"Goodbye, Matt!" Voices of people he could not see called out to him from the *Cardena* and because he could not see them, it seemed in the darkness that it was the ship itself that was saying goodbye.

Then he recognized Monica's voice. "Matt! Can you hear me?"

"Yes."

"Remember Matt, it's a return ticket. You don't have to stay if you don't want to."

"Don't stand up, and don't make any sudden moves," said his father. "You'll tip us and we'll drown, and even if we don't, I'll lose them boom chains. This little tub can't take the extra weight and I wasn't counting on a passenger."

A tin patch was nailed to the inside of the hull. Normally the patch would have been well above the waterline but the added weight of Matt and the boom chains had lowered the boat, and water was now pouring through the patch.

"Better start bailing!" said his father.

"What with?" asked the boy, searching the boat for an empty can or bottle.

His father reached under his seat, came up with a bottle of whiskey, unscrewed the cap, and, raising the bottle above his head, in a single motion quaffed the remaining liquor and handed the empty bottle to Matt. "This'll do the trick. Good thing I remembered I had it or we'd be sunk for sure."

Matt began to bail frantically.

XI

IN RIVERS INLET THE SOCKEYE salmon were beginning the final phase of their life, the journey up the Wannock River to spawn. The *Cardena* had crossed Queen Charlotte Sound and was loading salmon at the cannery in Shotbolt Bay. The "cannery run" portion of the trip had begun in earnest: seven canneries in Rivers Inlet, one at Namu, one at Lowe Inlet in Grenville Channel, twelve canneries on the Skeena River, and four on the Nass.

At the head of Rivers Inlet mountains rose abruptly from the inlet's floor and streams of fresh water poured down sheer, bare slopes into green, glacial water. Hundreds of gillnet skiffs from seven canneries were gathering to take the last catch of the sockeye season. A string of skiffs was towed to the fishing grounds, each boat twenty-five feet long: one man, his gillnet, and enough groceries for a week of hard, lonely labour. Cork floats of the nets were strung in all directions. In the evening each man marked the end of his net with a light, and the inlet was aglow with hundreds of lanterns.

"A beautiful floating city of lights," said Monica, watching from the deck of the *Cardena*.

But to Cameron each light represented a man, alone in an open boat, from Sunday night to the following Friday night, five whole days and nights without relief. He imagined each man dozing fitfully through the night, the water lapping at the sides of his round-bottom boat, and then, at dawn, wrestling his heavy, lead-weighted net into his boat, forcing each salmon backwards from the mesh that held it behind the gills.

Then the collector would come out and take the fish, and give him a chit to take to the cannery at the end of the week. But the part that Cameron couldn't get over was the price being paid for the catch. He had talked to the fishermen on the dock at Alert Bay, so he knew exactly what the canneries were paying.

Warehouse sheds were filled to capacity and cases of salmon were stacked on the docks. The canneries were begging ships like the *Cardena* to take their canned salmon to Vancouver, but the prices the fishermen were getting for their catch had hit rock bottom. Sockeye brought twenty-five cents apiece. Cameron couldn't believe it. A quarter for a whole sockeye salmon. Fishermen were getting twelve and a half cents for a whole coho, fifty cents apiece for red spring over ten pounds. But the price that sent Cameron and the fishermen on the dock reeling was the price of pinks. Two and a half cents each.

"Tell me," one of the fishermen had asked Cameron, "how you split a penny in half?"

Cameron thought about that and about what the old man in Kelsey Bay had said. The same salmon hanging in his smokehouse, that would feed him all winter, was fetching two and a half cents each in the commercial fishery. "I have no money but I'm rich," he had said.

The *Cardena* was capable of loading fifteen hundred cases of salmon in an hour, each case containing ninety-six half-pound cans.

When the ship completed her cannery run, she would return to Vancouver with tons of salmon in her hold. Someone was making money and it wasn't the fisherman out there alone in his boat all night, all week. The man out there with the light on the end of his net was, like the salmon he sought, caught in a trap, but unlike the salmon, it was a trap of his own devising.

And you, Cameron, he thought to himself, what trap have you set for yourself by throwing everything over to be at the side of a woman you know very little about, except that you can't be without her?

"Yes," he lied. "The lights are beautiful."

And they were, as long as you didn't think about their meaning or wonder where Matt was; Cameron and Monica were both worrying over the boy.

JUST BEFORE DAWN, the mail boat bumped against the pilings and Koko leapt onto the dock as Emily steadied herself. Ahead of her, the two men who ran the *Ida B* carried the mail bags and her bags, leading the way over the long, uneven floats that were strung together to make the dock. The sea rippled between each float so they had to walk on planks from one float to another.

She climbed a steep embankment while above her Koko, his face planted at the edge of the hill, looked down at her and waited. Then she was at the top, following the man with her bags through a gate, walking with Koko toward a boarding house verandah.

At the kitchen table, a woman was already sorting the mail. The lives Emily had wondered about earlier were being stacked in neat piles on her table, waiting to be received at this, their final destination.

And you? the woman seemed to say, peering over her glasses at Emily.

"Could you arrange a boat ride for me in the morning up the inlet to the Indian village, Quatsino?"

"Of course. But there won't be anyone there. Not this time of year. They're all salmon fishing."

"Oh, I don't mind," said Emily.

Walking ahead of Emily the woman opened the door to a room and set down her bag. What will a white middle-aged woman and her dog do in a deserted Indian village? she asked herself.

As soon as the door was shut, and without noticing anything about the room, Emily fell onto the bed for a few hours' sleep.

MATT SAT AT the stern of a boat so small that the slightest shift in his weight might capsize the precarious little craft. Each time his father brought up the oars he leaned forward toward the boy so that in the moment before he dipped the oars again their faces were inches apart and Matt could smell the liquor on his breath.

Is this what he had been searching for, what he had thought he needed so badly? Already he missed the *Cardena* and everyone onboard it. The ship was only a distant, receding light, then that too was snuffed out and he was alone in the darkness with this strange, wild creature across from him.

"Wait till Sarah meets you!" said Frank Clayton.

"Sarah?"

"My woman. You'll really like her," he enthused.

Matt was supposed to adjust to this new order of things. Well, he thought, what should he have expected?

His father gave one long, last, hard pull on the oars and the little skiff smacked up onto the shore. They wrestled the boom chains out of the boat, dragged them up the beach, and dropped them in the bush behind a log.

"Well, here we are!" said his father.

Yes, thought Matt. But where?

His father lit a candle that flared to life inside a tin can. "We'll need some light to see where we're going. Watch your footing. It's slippery here."

The wobbly candlelight flickered as they picked their way through the driftwood and seaweed toward a shack sitting on skid logs half afloat and held to the shore by a rusty cable wrapped around a stump.

Inside, a woman had fallen asleep in a chair in front of an oil drum stove in which the fire had gone out. When the door opened, she jumped out of the chair, startled.

Matt and the woman stared at each other.

"Who are you?" she demanded, pulling a blanket tight around her shoulders.

Matt wished he'd never found his father. Still, what had he imagined? That his father would live alone? But this, anything but this.

"I," he began, "I . . ."

"This is my son, Matthew. Matt, this is Sarah."

She was dark, with jet-black hair. Was she Indian or a half-breed? He didn't know and it didn't matter. She wasn't his mother, that's what mattered. When she sat next to his father, she placed the palm of her hand on his leg, above his knee.

They were seated thus, his arm around the woman's shoulder,

she leaning into him, her hand on his thigh, when Frank asked, "How's your mother these days?"

Matt was speechless. With a shock, he realized his father was unaware of his mother's death. How could he know? She'd only been in the ground a week.

"She's dead." The closeness of the tiny shack and the smoke from the newly built fire filled him with nausea. He bolted for the door and stepped outside into the dark, then stopped, for if he took another step he would fall off the floathouse into the sea. He was beginning to hate his father, the man he had searched and longed for.

"He'll get over this. I mean, you and me," Frank Clayton said to the woman. "Hell, he's just a kid." Then, added as an afterthought to himself, "I didn't know she was dead."

There was only one place for Matt to sleep, on the floor, and he did not sleep. Instead, he lay awake, longing for Cameron, Monica, the eccentric old lady who scribbled in notebooks and hastily fashioned incomprehensibly mysterious sketches she claimed were trees, and the whole crew of the *Cardena* who had adopted him as if he were their own son, and the ship itself, that inanimate object that somehow for him had taken on a life of its own, and in so doing, given him a life.

XII

EMILY HAD FALLEN ASLEEP EXHAUSTED a few hours before and now saw in the daylight that her room was filled with cigarette butts, dead flowers, matches and dirt on the floor, and dried vomit on the wall. The night's rough sea off Cape Scott had left her with a splitting headache compounded by the morning discovery of the dirty room. Thank God she had slept on the bed, not in it, she thought to herself. She stood up, holding onto the bureau to steady herself. What was she doing here?

Then she remembered. Earlier, she had asked the woman who rented her this horrid room about hiring a boat to take her to the Indian village of Quatsino.

She shut the door, taking her two bags with her so she would not have to return. She made her way downstairs to the kitchen but no one was there. At the end of the dock, a man waited for her in a fourteen-foot clinker rowboat with no name. She looked down into the open boat. Then she began to ease herself, Koko, and her bags into it. Of the vessels carrying her on her journey, the *Cardena*, the *Ida B*, and this one, this was the smallest. Here she did not look down at the sea from the height of a deck and railing. Here she could touch it. She dropped her hand over the side and felt the coolness of the water stream through her fingers.

It was the high season of the salmon fishery. On the fog-bound water hundreds of seabirds whooped and shrieked and dove into herring balls churned to the surface by feeding salmon. Emily listened to the cries of birds she could not see feeding in the fog.

"Hang on, ma'am. Here comes the beach!"

The fecund, sweet smell of seaweed rose from the shore to meet her. The keel crunched against the pebbles and the impact threw Emily forward out of her seat. Koko immediately jumped onto the beach. While Emily was still getting out, she was suddenly invaded by eight cats that leapt into the boat and surrounded her. They arched their backs and purred and waved their striped tails and rubbed against her legs as they followed her.

The tide was low, the seaweed on the rocks slippery underfoot. The fog was lifting, hovering over the cedar-plank houses at the edge of the shore, clinging to the treetops in the forest that rose behind.

Not a single boat on the beach nor a soul in sight. Stillness hung like the fog itself over the village. She listened to the distant cry of the birds. No one came out to greet her. Everyone was either out on their boats fishing or working in the cannery. Except for the cats, the village was deserted.

She began walking up the beach toward the totem poles that slanted skyward in front of a house in the centre of the bay. Two great sea lion house posts flanked the front door, supporting a carved cross-beam that in turn supported the ridgepole that ran the length of the house. Twin stylized sea lions with heavy rounded snouts and nostrils, and large squared teeth, stared at her through ovoid eyes. Carved in red cedar, they were weathered grey by sea winds, sand, and salt. Cracks opened like wounds in the beings carved there, vertical open lines that ran the length of the posts.

Next to the old plank house, a little clapboard house had been built, so new and soulless it could have been dropped out of an Eaton's catalogue. Behind this new house, in a clearing where once there had been a plank house, the fallen poles and massive house beams lay on the ground under a blanket of moss, the first reclaiming of the forest.

Change was everywhere. She could feel it in the fog lifting up into the trees. She could feel it in herself. Here where the land met the water, the stones worn smooth by the tumbling action of the waves, where everything was in a state of flux and change, it was possible to believe the transformation myths. Beings merged and changed into each other, and yes, perhaps all changed into one great being: the totems, the cedar houses, all engulfed by the forest that rose behind. Emily turned and began walking.

She was following a path across the field behind the village that led into the forest. The cats, all eight of them, leapt and darted on both sides of the path, the grass so tall all Emily saw was the curved ends of their striped tails as they moved with her into the forest.

XIII

THAT SAME MORNING, PASSENGERS ON the *Cardena* still sleeping were awakened by the blowing of the ship's whistle at exactly two-minute intervals. The fog that quartermaster Briggs feared and Wilson had foretold now enveloped the ship. Briggs gripped the wheel. Out the wheelhouse window he saw nothing, not even the bow of the ship, nothing but a blanket of white, obscuring fog. Beside him stood the captain, with his eyes closed, working the ship's whistle, steering blind.

They might survive, Briggs thought, in open sea, simply waiting for the fog to lift, but no, they were steaming Full Ahead Northwest from Wright Sound up Grenville Channel, a forty-five-mile-long channel that narrowed to less than a quarter of a mile between steeply forested canyon walls.

Monica and Cameron were the only passengers who ventured on deck. He could feel the dampness of the fog on her skin. The smell of the sea was in her hair. He heard the cries of unseen birds feeding in the current. The walls of the channel enclosed them, womb-like.

"When the fog lifts, it will be a beautiful day," said Cameron.

"How do you know?" she asked idly.

They were looking over the side of the ship, still aglow from a night of love, suspended, in the morning's fog.

"Fog in the morning means sun in the afternoon."

Already they could feel warmth piercing through the fog. It was dissipating now, a blue sky above and the white blanket that still hung stubbornly over the water's surface like a white cloud. Then, as they were gazing overboard, something hove into view, hallucinatory, surreal, as if they were flying low in an airplane just above the cloud line, where the peaks of mountains poke through, so too the peaks of rooftops, one, and then another, and another, poked above the white layer of fog that lay on the water.

A caravan of floathouses was being towed from one bay to another. Families scrambled out of their houses in panic as the bow of the *Cardena* bore down on them out of the fog. The ship swerved at the last minute, narrowly missing the float camp, the ship's wake washing against the houses.

Briggs had seen the rooftops poking through the fog.

"It was like you said, Wilson. He kept his eyes shut the whole time we were in the fog. I tell you I was so scared my legs shook while I was standing at the wheel, and then, just when he called out a fifteen-degree course change I seen rooftops above the fog ahead of us and I spun the wheel and we slid on by so close I saw the faces of the people on the floats and then they were lost in the fog and you know, that whole time, he never did open his eyes. Not once, not for a moment."

"What good would it have done to open his eyes? Can't see in the fog anyway. No, the skipper sees with the sound of the whistle."

Wilson had wanted to have a little fun with the new quartermaster when he first came aboard in Vancouver but the joke had gone far enough. It was time to set things straight.

"The reason the skipper shuts his eyes in the fog has to do with the echo of the ship's whistle. Here in Grenville Channel, he listens for which echo comes back first and changes the course a few degrees so he gets the echo back in about two seconds from each side. That's the way he keeps the ship in the middle of the channel, with the echo coming the same distance from each side. Sound travels a mile in five and a half seconds. If the echo takes eleven seconds, then he knows he's a mile off shore: five and a half seconds for the sound of the whistle to go ashore and five and a half seconds to come back. If he gets the whistle back in two seconds, he's less than a quarter mile off."

"So all the time he's listening for the echo," said Briggs, "counting the seconds, he's concentrating by keeping his eyes closed?"

"When the echo didn't come back at the right interval, he knew, without ever opening his eyes to see it, that there was another vessel in the channel, and so he called out that fifteen-degree course change. Boyce is the best there is. He brought this ship over from Glasgow and he's sailed into every nook and cranny on this coast. And believe me, I've sailed with some bad skippers too. On this very ship we had a relief skipper, and I was sitting right here in the officers' mess, waking up with a cup of coffee and eating hotcakes, waiting to go on watch, and I happened to glance sideways out a porthole and what did I see? The pilings of a dock whizzing by, and all I could do was run as fast as I could to the stern of the ship because that relief skipper was plowing Full Ahead into the dock, and you can bet the people standing on the dock were running for their lives. That man took out half the wharf. And what did he offer as an explanation? 'I rang for Full Astern and they gave me Full Ahead.' Tried to blame it on the engineer.

"That's another thing about Boyce. He doesn't blame anyone else. Takes full responsibility. Even took the heat when his first mate put the *Catala* aground on Sparrowhawk Reef. A ship with a crew that doesn't have confidence in its captain is not a good ship to be on, and believe me, Boyce is the best, and that's why this is the best ship in the fleet to be on."

FOR THE FIRST time since he had begun travelling on the Union steamships ten years ago, Cameron was not going to a job and had no specific destination, and for the first time too, he was seeing the coast through new eyes.

Ideas were forming inside his head so fast he couldn't keep track of them. He missed the obvious irony that he had travelled up a narrow body of water named Discovery Passage and at its northern end, Kelsey Bay, had experienced a series of revelations. It had all begun, his changed way of seeing things, when he encountered the old man in Kelsey Bay. He had left an impression so profound and complete Cameron was just beginning to digest it. In the simplest terms, he was living proof of the successful, self-sustaining life that could be lived on the coast.

Timber was left lying on the ground, worth nothing because it had no market value, and a whole salmon fetched two and a half cents. Yet he had seemed perfectly comfortable living off the land. What did it mean?

Cameron had been puzzling, turning over and over in his mind a single question, trying to find an answer. Whenever he thought of the cedar and the salmon, he kept returning to this central question: Did things have an intrinsic value or worth other than their market value?

Yes, he decided. As long as a person didn't try to sell the commodity but kept it for his own use. The successful existence of the man in Kelsey Bay was in itself proof. He knew, the Indians knew, and now Cameron knew. But what could he do with this knowledge now that he had absorbed it? What good was the cedar log the old man had uncovered beneath the moss at Kelsey Bay unless he had known what to do with it?

"You're so quiet," Monica said. "What are you thinking?"

The woman of his dreams lay in his arms. He wanted to build a cedar house and live in it with her but she was on her way to her mine manager at Anyox.

She turned and lay on top of him, looking into his eyes, and then, as if reading his mind, said, "Be glad for this time we have together. Let's make the most of it."

XIV

"C'MON, SON. LET'S GO LOGGING."

Matt hadn't slept all night and logging was the last thing on his mind. "Do you have any equipment?" he asked.

"We don't need much for this kind of logging, what we call hand logging. Nothing we don't have: a double-bladed axe, a crosscut saw, and a Gilchrist screw jack. Helps to have a peavey and we got that too."

They began to climb the steep face of a hillside that seemed to rise straight up out of the sea, his father clambering over stumps and the smashed debris of fallen trees while Matt tried to keep up. He was thankful when his father stopped ahead of him to catch his breath.

"There's two other pieces of equipment we need for hand logging I forgot to mention but you might have guessed."

"What are they?"

"A really steep hillside and gravity. We fall a tree on a grade like this and when it hits the ground, gravity and the grade give it a momentum that shoots it straight down the hill into the salt chuck."

Matt looked down the dizzying height of the hillside, a ramp of rock, stumps, bush, and raw earth. It was just as Shakey Jake had described it, but with one big difference: it was he, Matt, on that hillside and he was surprised by his father's inclusion of him in this madness. He had wanted to find him, to be with him, but Frank Clayton was avoiding any real encounter or communication by throwing himself and his son into gruelling work.

He had stashed his tools under a stump at the edge of a stand of old-growth cedar halfway up the side of the mountain. Today he had brought an extra axe for the boy and there were even two metal-tipped springboards to set in the notches he would cut above the butt-swell where the diameter of the tree narrowed and there would be less wood to cut through.

The cedar was over six feet in diameter, so that standing on their springboards on either side of the giant tree, Matt and his father couldn't see each other. They balanced precariously on their narrow platforms, father and son wielding double-bladed axes filed razor sharp.

All day they worked to fall that single tree. The procedure was the same as Matt had witnessed in Port Hardy—the undercut to determine the direction of the fall, followed by the back cut. But this time it was all done by hand. Lunch consisted of some hastily eaten bannock. Sometime in the afternoon, they axed out the undercut, moved to the back of the tree, and began the back cut with the two-handled crosscut saw. An hour later, Matt had to wrap a rag around the saw handle to staunch the flow from the blisters breaking into bleeding sores on the palms of his hands.

"Now you know why we call this saw the misery whip."

Matt bent his back to the pull of the saw.

"Keep your eye on the cut!" called his father from the other end of the saw. "The instant we see our cut begin to widen, we back the saw out quick and jump off our boards. Make sure you have a good exit path because when this baby lets go, it'll be too late to look for one."

Late that afternoon the saw cut widened perceptibly and Matt sensed a slight movement overhead. Something stirred hundreds of feet above him. The mass of the tree was moving, tons of living matter coming unhinged from its base.

"Jump!" yelled his father.

As the tree toppled, they dove for cover, cowering in the underbrush. A hail of green cedar cones and broken branches fell around them. The tree crashed to the ground and immediately slid down the hillside. It hit the water with such force that its immense weight and momentum drove it under the surface where it disappeared for what seemed, as Matt and his father stood staring down the hillside after it, a full minute before it suddenly leapt vertically out of the water.

"Whowee!" whooped Matt's father and slapped his son on the back. "Now we're logging!"

Matt looked down the hillside at the broken debris and gouged-out earth plowed in the path of the fallen tree that now floated dead in the water below them.

"WHAT DO THESE forests make you feel?" Emily wrote in her journal.

She looked up into the forest canopy where Sitka spruce needles combed the fog, trapping the moisture that hung in droplets from the tip of each blue-green branch high above her.

The sun probed the fog in shafts of light that slanted between the trees and fell onto the forest floor in a patch of brightness where the cats settled in around Emily, Koko at her feet. She began to unpack her sketchbook and charcoal, thinking, so many journeys, never for their own sake. Each had a purpose connected to her art, each was a passage through a stage of development in her art. She had painted a visual record of Northwest Coast Indian art, yet this art could have its full effect only on people familiar with the stories and concepts that lay behind it, and to this she would always be an outsider.

Her great coastal journeys were already behind her, a six-week expedition travelling alone in 1912 to Alert Bay, then up the Skeena to the Gitksan villages and on to the Queen Charlotte Islands and the villages of the Haida. In 1928 she returned to the Charlottes and sketched in the rain the abandoned village of Skedans, and on that same trip went up the Skeena and Nass rivers. The next year, 1929, Nootka and Friendly Cove, and now Quatsino. What would she discover here she had not already found?

"For a while, at least, give up the Indian motifs," her friend and mentor, Lawren Harris, had advised her. "Perhaps you have become too dependent on them; create forms for yourself, direct from nature."

If each trip had a purpose, what was the purpose of this, her latest and, already she knew, her last voyage north? And why here? She could easily have stayed onboard the *Cardena* and continued north up the Skeena and Nass, but she had planned on going to Quatsino.

There was the real journey and the one in her mind. Captain Boyce had shown her how he recorded the ship's passage, entering notations of time, tide, bearing, and speed in his logbook. As the ship made its way through the morass of islands and inlets, recording ten navigation changes in ten minutes wasn't unusual. Then, when the ship had to run the same route in the dark, or when visibility was poor, the captain could follow the course set out by the previous passage. As long as the speed was constant, the same course and time could be used over and over. Boyce sometimes augmented his terse notations with sketches of mountaintops, islands, and prominent landmarks that might help him find his way. They weren't bad either, as she remembered them.

But how was she to find *her* way? She was in an unknown place, a place she had never been before.

She sat among some of the largest and oldest living things the earth has ever created. Emily looked up into the gauze-like canopy, where the sun filtered through fog and the thin uppermost tips of the delicate, tender, new growth.

An eagle settled into the top of a tall snag. The big bird shifted its weight on its branch and studied the cats, the dog, and the woman below. The cats were a familiar part of the eagle's territory but the dog and the woman were not.

"My aims are changing," she wrote in her journal. "I feel lost and perplexed." She was fifty-nine years old yet it seemed she was still learning, discovering new techniques, new vision. Her trip to Quatsino Sound has taken her to the centre of Vancouver Island, the island she was born on; it was a journey of changing perceptions.

XV

THE DAY'S WORK WAS NOT finished when Matt and his father fell the tree that lay floating in the water at the foot of the mountain. They scrambled down the steep grade, rowed out, and began axing off the limbs. The tree was so big that even with its branches lopped off, they could hardly tow it to the log boom Frank Clayton was assembling beyond his floathouse.

It was dusk when they finally secured the log to the boom and tied the rowboat to the floathouse. A stew of deer meat simmered on the oil drum wood stove inside. Sarah made a mattress out of cedar boughs piled on the floor and after a supper of stew and fried bread, Matt collapsed from fatigue onto the makeshift bed. He lay on his back and stared up into the rough-hewn rafters, wondering why his father had chosen to forsake him and his mother for a life such as this. He had come all this way to find his father, the father he yearned for, and he *had* found him. Yet they had talked of nothing and now, drifting into sleep, Matt felt farther away from him than ever.

THE NEXT DAY, perched on springboards, two strangers, a father and his son, chopped out the undercut on another giant cedar. The girth of the tree was so great that a single set of notches for the springboards did not suffice. Instead, they had to work their way around the circumference of the tree with a series of springboard notches.

Axe strokes echoed down the hillside and across the water. A mound of fresh wood chips grew at the base of the doomed tree. Each stroke seemed to ratchet up the tension between father and son till Matt was wound tight with frustration.

When the undercut was complete, they began the back cut, wielding the long, two-handled crosscut saw. The exertion and coordination demanded of Matt and his father as they worked together to fall the tree precluded conversation. Matt wondered if his father had thrown them into this work to avoid communicating with a son he had abandoned and not seen for over a year.

There was a momentary release of this tension when the tree let go, but instead of careening down the hillside into the water below, as on the previous day, the huge tree stopped dead halfway down the hillside.

"Helluva note!" cursed Frank. "Now we're in for it!"

Yes, thought Matt. A hell of a note. To come this far, for what? To stand and stare at a fallen tree halfway down a hillside? And what had he expected? He had been following his mother's instructions. Still, he wished he could talk to her now, for he felt she had kept something from him. How many years had they been separated? He pondered, thinking over his father's absence.

"Yes," he said, repeating his father's words. "It's a hell of a note. What do we do now?"

"Cut away the branches holding the tree back. Plan an escape route or we'll be crushed or swept into the water when the tree starts to slide down the hillside. We'll have to get the jack and peavey and use the jack to take the weight off the log so we can roll it free." If the jack let go, the tree could roll back and crush them, and if the tree rolled free, they would have to dive out of the way fast.

"Be careful, son."

It was his father's use of the word *son* that caused Matt to break.

"Since when did you ever care about what happens to me!" He kicked violently at the fallen tree. The giant cedar rolled off the jack, broke free, and skidded down the hill.

Stunned into silence, they both stared after it and then began to pick their way down the hill. When they reached the beach Matt raged on. "How could you leave us? Have you any idea what her life was like? How she had to scrape and borrow just to keep us alive? And for what?"

"This won't work, son. You can't do this. She's dead and we're alive. I'm sorry, but that's the way it is."

"Why did you leave?"

"I . . . I . . . look, I'm a logger, that's all."

"More like you ran out on her." Matt shot the words at his father with a force and directness that surprised even himself and then, for the first time, confronted the truth. "And me too," he blurted. "You ran out on me too."

His wife had cut off his access to their son but he could not bear to tell the boy this.

He said, "That's not true. I had to move up the coast to go logging."

"That's what you do, isn't it? You cut down living things and then you move on to some other place. You killed her."

"You don't know what you're talking about. She died of cancer."

"Why?" Matt screamed into the empty, unanswering mountains. "Why?"

He was beyond reason, blinded by tears and rage. He looked up at the debris and broken branches where the fallen tree had skidded down the hill. "Why did you do this?"

He meant not only the scarred wreckage of the hillside but also the destroyed marriage of his mother and father.

His father shrugged. "Because it's here, I guess. The forest."

"That's no reason."

"You don't understand. It *is* here, right here, a steep slope, the sea at the bottom. It's all a hand logger like me has to work with. You know, I could use some help here. Father and son, working together. You and me. We get these logs in the water, come out of this depression with a bankroll, form a company, a small outfit, just one truck. I can see it now painted on the side of the cab door: FRANK CLAYTON AND SON LIMITED, LOGGING. What do you think?"

It was the farthest thing from Matt's mind and all he could do was shake his head in wonder.

"I take it that's no for an answer but know what I think?"

"No. I haven't the . . ." Matt began.

"I think you're scared of the work. You can't cut it. You haven't the nerve, the guts for it."

"Maybe," Matt said. "But maybe it's not whether I've got the guts for it. Maybe it's more like I've got too many brains for it."

"What's that supposed to mean?"

"It seems a simple-minded, stupid activity."

"Why you gutless little wonder!"

Frank grabbed Matt by his shoulders and threw him down on the beach. The smooth round pebbles gave easily under him, so that he was more startled than hurt, but Matt knew then that he had to get away.

XVI

COLD. EVEN IN THIS AFTERNOON sun, Monica's hands on the white enamelled railing were cold, as the *Cardena* glided silently through the narrow passage of green water halfway up Grenville Channel. Its rock walls rose straight out of the sea on either side of the ship. A waterfall tumbled down the granite face into the salt water below. The ship passed so close to it that Monica, standing at the stern on the main deck, felt the spray on her face.

Matt had left the ship in the middle of the night. If she hadn't been wakened by the boom chains being dragged down the ramp, she might have missed him altogether. As it was, all she could do was call out to him from the *Cardena*, for by the time she dressed and came on deck he was already in the tiny rowboat with his father.

She missed Matt and she didn't know why. Perhaps it was his innocence. He had his whole life ahead of him and, of course, it was wonderful that he'd found his father.

Her eyes followed the trail of propeller backwash as it unwound behind the ship in churning white eddies down the narrow corridor of water whence the ship had come. As long as she stood at the centre of the railing and could look back and see that narrow passageway, she was all right. There must always be a way out.

"If you could see me now." She said this out loud, though there was no one near her on the rear deck. In her imagination she was calling out to her old lover, Bill Chalmers. "If you could see me now."

She didn't blame him, really. It was his father. After all these years, she could still feel his silent, steely stare across the Sunday dinner table. Without uttering a word, his look seemed always to ask, "And what, exactly, do *you* think *you* are doing here?"

Then the words of Bill Chalmers that ended everything. "Dad wants me to go to Princeton in the fall."

It was his father, she knew it.

"I guess we won't be seeing much of each other. I mean, I'll be in a dormitory thousands of miles from here."

She hadn't known what to say, and looking back on it now, after all these years, maybe it wasn't just the father, but the son, who should have stood up to his father but instead had bowed to his wishes. In the end it didn't matter which one she blamed; the experience changed the way she perceived men. She became watchful, predatory. She would take her revenge on all of them. Stuart Jenkins was only the latest in a long list.

All she wanted was peace and security but she knew you didn't get that with love. Love was a blind, consuming obsession. It had a momentum of its own, like the ship itself, always moving, even as she stood perfectly still on its deck. The ship moved under the direction of Captain Boyce, but she herself was moving without direction in unknown, uncharted waters. It was not a good feeling.

When she was young she could afford to be in love, but after she'd been broke a few times, really broke, and broken-hearted too, well then, she didn't want love anymore; she wanted security, and security was Stuart Jenkins at Anyox. Still, her body had an almost inexpressible need, a yearning for comfort that she knew the older man could not provide, a yearning that had driven her to seek out Cameron.

Most men were not good lovers. They wanted satisfaction but when they sensed or discovered their inadequacy they tried to compensate with gifts. Mutual knowledge of this inadequacy meant there was a point upon which she could control the man, and Monica was used to this position of power and control. Men did her bidding.

But with Cameron she had no control. Nor, for that matter, did he, for he had not left the *Cardena* at Port Hardy; he couldn't leave her, wouldn't leave her.

What had she done? What had she started? Cameron was a natural lover, not from experience but out of discovery and a desire to please. It amazed her that she could even think of letting something so wonderful go. But she must. For a few seconds, no more, a blink of the eyes, she acknowledged the hurt and pain she would cause him, and when she opened her eyes her gaze had dropped from the channel behind the boat straight down into the seething white water foaming from the propeller.

Ahead, the passage took a right-angle jog to starboard and Boyce quickly directed the *Cardena* through it. When Monica looked up, the familiar passageway she had seen from the stern had vanished. In its place a wall of mountains rose above the ship. The mountains closed in, as if the ship were sailing into them. She felt claustrophobic. The land crowded in on either side as if to seize the ship, to seize her.

She thought she was going one way and then, in the blink of an eye, she was going another.

XVII

AVOID PERILS. MANY WERE CHARTED and could be navigated through, others remained uncharted. Uncharted perils. As captain, and before, as first mate, and before then, as deckhand, Boyce, now in his senior years of service, had observed and catalogued these uncharted perils, which he characterized as the three Ls. Singly, each was a problem; combined, they could be deadly. Loggers, liquor, and ladies had wreaked havoc on many a Union ship.

The way Boyce saw it, people went nuts onboard a ship, got loose from their moorings, so to speak. And the loggers, who could blame them? They knew where they were going so they drank. The unlucky ones made the return trip as a corpse under the canvas cover of a lifeboat.

They even had their own ship, known up and down the coast as The Logger's Palace, the *Cassiar*, a wooden-hulled two-master converted to steam.

In the solitude of the *Cardena*'s wheelhouse, Boyce had only to close his eyes to see the pure, clean lines of the *Lady Alexandra*, the largest excursion ship north of San Francisco, under a full head of steam, triple-expansion engines pushing the ship through the water at fourteen knots, bunting snapping in the wind, every inch of the deck crowded with passengers.

She was licensed to carry fourteen hundred, but the night he, as first mate, took over from a drunken skipper there must have been two thousand onboard because at midnight, when the ship's whistle sounded, they used five gangplanks to get them all onboard, and then, as the ship backed off Bowen Island, some fully clothed fool dove off the bow and swam back to the wharf right in front of Boyce's eyes, while a band on the bridge played "The End of a Perfect Day." Insanity, a floating loony bin: couples screwing in the lifeboats, people sick and vomiting, depressed and crying. A man tried to kill himself. A woman crawled underneath the bridge and got stuck; she was left there until they docked in Vancouver.

Master of this chaos was a small man with gigantic ears and an enlarged, pitted red nose, Captain Fred Bates, much given to drink himself, so much so that on the night in question he couldn't dock the ship on the return to Vancouver. Instead, he had First Mate Boyce take the controls in the wheelhouse while, for the sake of appearances, he went out on the bridge and posed with a second telegraph.

In the midst of this pantomime, Boyce worked the telegraph that brought the ship safely to dock and thought, I'm doing the captain's job so I might as well write for my master's ticket and get paid for doing it.

Tourists. Excursionists. On the tourist-laden southern boats Boyce had to shave every morning and be properly dressed, and he dared not spit over the wheelhouse rail. Luckily, there were very few excursion passengers who took the entire return trip on the *Cardena*'s northern cannery run. True, on this trip there was Cameron, and the woman, Monica James, but the couple seemed to live from moment to moment, hardly knowing where they were. One day, Cameron was getting off in Port Hardy, the next day he was on for the duration of the trip. The Carr woman would be waiting in Port Hardy, but he hardly considered her an excursion passenger or tourist. She had been travelling north to the Indian villages for over twenty years now to sketch the totems, the people, the forest. What was it she saw that others didn't see? No, she was certainly no ordinary tourist or excursion passenger.

Thank God when he got his captain's ticket the company put him on the northern route where he provided a real service. Truth was, those isolated villages, float camps, canneries, and sawmills couldn't exist without the Union steamships. Or was it the other way round? The Union steamships couldn't exist without the communities. In the first year of what everyone was calling a depression, as business fell off, the Union was planning to cut back on its northern sailings during the winter.

On a late-night watch with no one in the wheelhouse but himself and the quartermaster, the captain let his mind wander; he hadn't finished with the three Ls yet. Had he missed anything? There didn't seem to be any trouble on this trip with loggers and liquor, but then he remembered the two Swedes who had been in the bar since the *Cardena* left Port Hardy. They had already picked a fight with their boss, the chainsaw salesman, Stanley Shanks. They would bear watching, those two.

And the third L was the truly uncharted deepest of mysteries, the ladies. Oh yes, he had seen Monica James on his ship before, and Cameron too, but Cameron had gone to the purser and purchased passage for the rest of the trip.

"On for the duration, then," Boyce had said to the purser when he learned of this development.

"It seems so. A rough ride." The purser paused, looked at Boyce, and added, "The weather, you know." But both men knew they were speaking of Monica.

"Well, we accomplished one good thing this trip," said the purser. "The boy is with his father."

"Yes," said Boyce. "Thanks to your sharp eye on the freight invoices."

They gazed out the wheelhouse window at a night sea and imagined the boy with his father.

XVIII

MATT WAS TRYING TO REMEMBER what Monica had shouted to him from the *Cardena*, something about a return trip ticket. But he had no way of knowing where the *Cardena* was, nor where he was. He had found his father but he knew he must get away from him. He had not come all this way to be thrown down on a beach by his own father.

He undid the rope, eased himself onto the plank seat in the centre of the small boat, and pushed it free from the floathouse. He let the boat drift, careful not to make any noise. As the boat floated farther away from the shore, he realized he had no food or water. He hadn't thought this out at all. He knew only that he had to get away.

Afterward, he would say to himself, I just needed to get away for a while, row off some anger, but I rowed too far, and got lost.

The best, the *only* thing he could do was take each moment step by step, stroke by stroke. The dry leather of the oarlocks creaked across the silence of the bay as he bent to the rhythm of the oars. Small eddies pushed from each dip of the blades lengthened into a parallel twin trail receding behind the moving stern, as his father's floathouse diminished in the growing distance. Hypnotic, mesmerizing, the oars churned tiny phosphorescent fragments of light in the dark water. He had to stay awake. Why? What had he now to stay awake for? Nothing.

Matt nodded off, oars trailing idle in the water. The boat in which he fell asleep became, in his dreams, the boat of his youth, the boat he and his father had fished in. The skiff slid through the dark void, the oars hung from the oarlocks, and Matt dreamt in fits and starts that he was a boy again, wild and free on Vancouver Island.

Like a leaf or a twig caught in the current, the skiff moved without direction. One moment the little boat's bow was pointed one way and then it was caught in an eddy and swirled so it was completely turned around.

MATT WAKENED WITH a chill, water soaking into his boots. Time to start bailing. At least he had replaced his father's empty whiskey bottle with a proper bailing can. The physical exertion of bailing, rowing, keeping the rhythm, dipping the blades, pushing against the water kept him from thinking.

Oars stilled, suspended just above the water, drops fell from the tips of the blades into the sea. Where was he? Where was he going? Darker than the night, the distant silhouette of an island was visible, and on its shore a dim, flickering light.

It was now September and three Kwakiutl women were taking advantage of the low night tide to harvest the first of the fall clams. A torch, fashioned from cedar bark and spruce pitch, provided a light for them to work by. They were aided in this task by two boys and a small black dog.

The women dragged their yew-wood rakes through the sand and eel grass. The boys knelt in the sand, sifting the murky seawater that pooled in the trench, their fingers feeling for the clams. The dog busied itself pawing at the tiny air holes in the sand out of which the clams would suddenly spray arcs of seawater. Around and around the dog ran madly while all about it erupted little geysers. When the dog tired of this, it stuck its snout into the trench, shook the water from its soaked fur, and waited for the boys to toss it damaged clams, their shells broken by the women's rakes.

Matt began rowing toward the light from the clam diggers' torch, only to find his boat caught in a kelp bed just offshore. This, he decided, was not a bad thing, for the voices that came across the water were not speaking English. The people on the beach were Indians. He would simply curl himself up against the cold and wait for them to leave.

The dog was elsewhere now, wading in water up to its belly and barking furiously. Ignoring the animal, the clam diggers continued to fill their baskets, their time limited by the tide, which was now turning, and the light left in their torch. They were not alarmed by the dog. It would bark at anything: a log floating free from a broken boom, a seal or sea lion breaking the surface, even the dark bulbs of kelp bobbing just offshore.

Baskets filled, the women began to make their way back to the village, but when they called the dog it would not come. Burdened with the weight of the clams, the women had no patience for the dog and continued on, but the boys, curious, stayed behind and walked to the water's edge where the dog barked unceasingly.

Then they saw it. Not a dugout or a canoe, but a white man's boat, abandoned, empty, and caught in the kelp bed. They looked at each other, whooped with delight, hugged their dog, and told it how good it was. Truly the sea was, as their elders said, a great provider. They had only to wade out to the boat and it would be theirs.

"Hey!" With a jerk Matt sat up, startled awake by being pulled through the kelp.

The boys had found more than a boat, and in that sudden moment of recognition and realization, it was hard to know who was more surprised and frightened. But there were two of them and they were in the land and waters of the Kwakiutl. They quickly pulled the boat forward until it slammed against the shore, throwing the white interloper onto the beach.

XIX

THE *CARDENA* WAS APPROACHING THE Skeena River by way of Telegraph Passage, a narrow body of water defined by the mainland to starboard, and Kennedy and then De Horsey Island on the port side. As the ship entered the mouth of the Skeena River, it passed, on the south shore of Kennedy Island, the place from which it took its name: Cardena Bay, after Captain García López de Cárdenas.

In the wheelhouse Boyce concentrated on keeping his ship in deep water. With his head out the wheelhouse window, he listened for the sound of sand scraping against the hull. Twice last winter he had run aground in the Skeena. Heavy siltation in the estuary meant the bottom was always changing, the mid-channel fairway shifting.

It was his worst nightmare: his beloved *Cardena*, flagship of the fleet, lay on its side on a sandbar in the Skeena River slough near the North Pacific Cannery. That was in November 1929. Passengers and freight were taken off and a salvage ship arrived from Prince Rupert. Two days later they pulled the ship free and floated it. Then on the *Cardena*'s first trip north after being repaired, on December 19, 1929, Boyce went aground again on Village Island in the Skeena River. To his everlasting shame, someone took a photograph of the *Cardena* high and dry, and distributed it up and down the coast as a postcard.

Two groundings within a month last winter; he couldn't afford a third, and now there was another hazard; the fishermen, a maze of gillnet boats, nets strung across the estuary, blocked his passage. He had to get through, had to find the mid-channel fairway and stay in it. If he altered his course to avoid snagging a gillnet, he ran the risk of running aground again. The *Cardena* needed sixteen feet of water to stay afloat, and on the Skeena, every inch of water meant the difference between being afloat or high and dry on a sandbar.

As if they too could somehow foresee or direct the successful forward progress of his ship, a group of men gathered on the forward main deck and gazed anxiously ahead at the maze of gillnetters' boats scattered across the grey-brown water of the estuary.

"Everything all right, skipper?" It was his first mate, Allan Grayson.

"No. It is not. Look at those silly buggers!" Boyce pointed at the boats dead ahead. "Give them the whistle. Five short blasts. If they don't move we'll go right on through them."

Grayson worked the whistle, counting to five between each blast, thinking there wouldn't be enough time for them to bring in their nets, even if they wanted to move.

"Hate to run them down, sir. In a way, they're our customers."

"If they won't move, cut the engines at the last minute and with any luck their nets will pass under our hull and miss the propellers. Do not, I repeat, do not alter our course."

Briggs was at the wheel. Everything he knew of navigation told him to avoid collision with another vessel, and now, as the *Cardena* bore down on the first of the little boats blocking their passage, his hands froze fast in panic to the wheel.

The men at the bow on the *Cardena*'s deck looked down at a fisherman in rubber boots and oilskins who shook his fist and shouted a stream of obscenities.

"You bastards! You've torn my net!"

Boyce rang for Stop Engines and the *Cardena* slid over the fisherman's net. Cork floats bobbed and danced and then were pulled under the hull of the ship as its wake threatened to capsize the fishboat.

Boyce rang for Slow Ahead. They weren't out of it yet.

"It could have been worse," said Wilson.

Though he was off watch, Wilson had come into the wheelhouse to encourage the new quartermaster, whose quick reaction, when Boyce ordered the course alteration, had prevented the *Cardena* from colliding with the floathouses in the fog in Grenville Channel.

"At night the moon throws a shadow on all those fishing boats with their nets out, and you don't know which side of their lights to stay on. One night, whoever was in one of those fishboats must've been asleep. I could hear all the pots and pans as we went past, all getting knocked around. That's how close we were."

"I doubt you were any closer than we were just now," said Briggs.

"Maybe so, but you saw how that fisherman wore big boots and oilskins?"

Briggs nodded.

"Well, last summer we hit a fishing boat. We didn't exactly hit her, we ran alongside of her, just like today. We were going slow, but the net, instead of sliding under our hull, tightened up on our bow and threw the fisherman overboard. We got the lifeboat out on the davits and down in the water, but by the time we got back to him, he was drowned. Didn't stand a chance wearing that heavy gear. He was expected to be a father in another week's time. So you see, it can always be worse."

The quartermasters fell silent, not wanting to talk of mishaps in the presence of the ship's two senior officers.

Now that they had gotten through the flotilla of gillnetters, Boyce still had to worry about running aground. "Break out the lead line and find the deckhand who can throw it farthest out from the bow," he said.

"That'd be Soogie Phelps," said Grayson.

Boyce went out on the bridge.

Passengers on the main deck made way for the deckhand carrying a coiled line. Phelps stood at the extreme forward bow and hurled the weighted line as far ahead of the ship as he could. When the weighted end hit the bottom he began quickly pulling the line in until his fingers closed on the three strips of leather tied to the line, and he shouted up to Boyce on the bridge, "Three fathoms! Three fathoms!"

He immediately coiled the line for another throw. The *Cardena* needed sixteen feet of water to stay afloat and at three fathoms, a depth of eighteen feet, the ship had only two feet of water between it and the river bottom. The trick was to get into the canneries on a high tide, load the salmon cases from one cannery, and then move on to the next cannery before the tide dropped.

WAITING BELOW FOR the whistle to blow to announce they would dock at the Claxton Cannery, Springline McLean and the winch man played cards on a pine coffin. The coffin was empty and made a fine card table. They had no idea who it was intended for.

Springline picked three cards off the makeshift table, studied them, and discarded two.

The winch man said, "Skipper says, 'When I come alongside you only got two slings of freight. I'll stop the derricks on this corner and get the freight off and I'll slide up and expect you to be at the other end with the empties. Just leave the boards there. Get the empties out of the other corner.' He told me, 'You got to sharpen up.' Boy, I thought I was running as hard as I could!"

Both men knew what was in store for them. They had to quickly unload freight and load thousands of cases of salmon, just so they could make the tide. If they didn't, they would lose their time off in Vancouver because the *Cardena* had to keep to its schedule. Now, in the final minutes before docking at the Claxton Cannery, they were trying to figure out whether they could count on any extra hands to help them load the salmon.

"Where's Phelps?"

"Soogie's above deck throwing a line for the old man so we won't get stuck in the mud."

"Grayson will help us. He always does. Then there's the quarter-masters."

"What about the kid?"

"The day man left us."

"I must have been off watch."

"Left in the middle of the night. Found his father."

"His father! Hell, he'd have been better off staying with us!" said Springline.

"Wonder where he is now?" The winch man threw his cards down on the coffin. "Maybe he's sitting around the fire all chummy pals with his dad."

"He should have stayed with us," insisted Springline. "I don't have a family and you don't either. The closest thing we got to family is the crew, ourselves, the boat. We accepted the boy, and now he's gone, snuck out on us in the dead of night without even a goodbye. I'm telling you, he should have stayed with us."

"For what? Working thirty-six hours straight for sixty-five dollars a month? You call this a life?"

Springline loved the ship and he loved being at sea. When they tied up in Vancouver he didn't get off the *Cardena* because being on land made him insecure, especially the dives around Hastings and Cordova where the *Cardena* docked. He lived onboard; it was the only life he knew. "Rumour is," he said, "when the cannery season ends, the Union plans to cut back their winter schedule on account of this depression, so you won't be able to bitch about your job because you won't have one."

The whistle blew, signalling the *Cardena*'s imminent docking at the Claxton Cannery.

"That's us. Time to hit the deck."

Springline pinched off the end of his cigarette, dropped the butt in his shirt pocket, and scrambled up the stairs and out the fo'c'sle hatch onto the main deck. You couldn't afford to waste tobacco. Last winter they went aground in the Skeena and the whole crew ran out of tobacco. They went nuts. Smoked tea leaves and the leavings off the wheelhouse deck where Wilson, the quartermaster, rolled his cigarettes in the dark on his midnight-to-six watch.

The *Cardena* slid alongside the cannery dock and Springline stood on the forward deck, glancing up at the bridge, waiting for Boyce's orders to throw the line for which he had earned his nickname. Once the lines were made fast the real work began. The Claxton Cannery had fifteen hundred cases of salmon to load, the first of the dozen cannery stops on the Skeena.

No onlookers loitered on the deck now. Both winches whirred and whined, engines hissing as the steel cables wound and unwound on their drums and the derricks swung from the dock to the deck, dropping their pallet loads into the holds forward and aft.

Wilson worked the forward winch, and the regular winch man worked the levers on the aft deck winch. Below, in the fore and aft holds, Springline McLean and Soogie Phelps manhandled the cases, each containing ninety-six half-pound cans, weighing almost fifty pounds. Briggs pitched in.

On the last trip out a load of coal had been delivered on the river and the hold had not been swept clean. Springline had lost his sense of smell when he was gassed in the First World War, but he knew coal dust when he saw it: black motes rising through the open hatch that turned the shaft of probing sunlight a sickening grey. In the heat of the hold the dust clung to the sweat on his neck. He unfolded his handkerchief and fashioned a crude mask to cover his mouth and nose.

"Hey! What the hell is going on down there?" yelled the winch man above deck when Springline paused.

Hell is right, thought Springline, and hurried to unfasten the winch man's load, bloody hell.

Boyce had timed the loading. With both winches and all hands working they had loaded fifteen hundred cases in thirty-five minutes; it was a good beginning, but only the start of the Skeena River cannery run.

Out of Claxton Cannery the *Cardena* steamed north up Telegraph Passage to Carlisle Cannery, where the gruelling schedule of loading cases of canned salmon was repeated. Briggs worked the aft hold with Springline and got his taste of the coal dust. As the *Cardena* left Carlisle Cannery and Briggs stepped through the varnished mahogany side door into the wheelhouse, Boyce took one look and sent him below for a shower.

"Can't have you up here in my wheelhouse looking like a coal miner," he said and took the wheel himself. There was a gleam in his grey eyes as he rang for Slow Ahead and spun the wheel in his hands. He was master of his ship and it felt good to handle the wheel.

When Briggs returned to the wheelhouse and relieved his captain, he noticed the course he was steering was no longer north but north by northeast. Then off the north end of De Horsey Island, Boyce called for another course change. "East," he said.

As was always the custom, the quartermaster repeated the course change back to the captain. "East," Briggs said, and began turning the wheel, watching the compass points spin before him as the ship came about.

WHERE WAS CAMERON? wondered Monica. She stood on the deck of the *Cardena*, which was now sailing east up a river, east into the mountains. She gripped the railing and stared into the snow-capped mountains in the distance, the land closing in on her again. Dead ahead, about a mile away, blue mountains rose straight out of the water, shrouded in mist, as the ship made a course change even more disturbing than the blind turn in Grenville Channel. She wanted only for her trip to be over, to arrive safely at the copper mine.

EVEN THOUGH THE Skeena was the largest river in British Columbia north of the Fraser, Boyce, the most seasoned of mariners, was uncomfortable on it. You never knew what would happen. Sternwheelers had plied the Skeena until the railway came through. They could navigate some one hundred miles upstream, to near Terrace, but the names the old-timers gave to its more difficult passages told the tale of the river's turbulence: Hardscrabble Rapids; Devils Elbow, where the river flowed straight into a rocky bluff and turned sharp at a right angle; the Hornet's Nest, at which the entire river was studded with submerged boulders; the Whirly Gig, a short, crooked passage through rocky walls with cross-currents, where boats danced and sidestepped.

True, these passages were upstream from where the *Cardena* ventured and some of them, like Hardscrabble Rapids, could be negotiated only with a cable to shore and a capstan pulling the boat. Then too, the sternwheelers were flat-bottomed riverboats, and the *Cardena* was no riverboat.

Like most men, Boyce had gone to sea for the freedom of it, to get away from the land, but on the river, he felt the land was about to swallow him up. There were deadheads, logs so waterlogged they were almost entirely submerged in a vertical position. Hit one and it would damage the hull or destroy a propeller. He only had to look at the shore and see the pilings, almost completely out of the water, to know how shallow it was. Hell, you could see the bottom, ugly grey sand and gravel. Stay in the fairway, stay in mid-channel, he told himself, but the channel was always changing, shifting with the silt, and there were no charts of the river.

He blew the ship's whistle, five blasts, a warning to the maze of boats ahead that he was coming through. It didn't matter whether you were on the Fraser or the Skeena, a river was always congested with traffic: towboats pulling barges and log booms; gillnet boats, haywire little outfits that knew nothing of marine navigation or right of way, but then, why should they? They weren't on the open sea; they were on the river.

The *Cardena* had loaded in Port Essington, and Boyce was about to make his turn to begin going downstream when a towboat began crossing in front of him. It was a wood-hulled steamer with a high, rounded wheelhouse and a low, long afterdeck with very little free-board. The towboat was crossing the *Cardena*'s bow so close Boyce could read the name lettered on the side, *Fearless*. More like *Stupid*, thought Boyce, and rang for Stop Engines. The *Cardena* waited for the tug to pass, Briggs steadying the ship in midstream, Boyce curs-ing the lost time.

Though the towboat had safely crossed the *Cardena*'s bow, the real problem lay some one hundred feet behind it, the tow itself. It was a barge loaded with logging equipment: a steam donkey engine, an A-frame, a bunkhouse, and a truck. The barge and its cargo far exceeded the size and tonnage of the towboat attempting to pull it across the river.

To give the barge more freedom of movement in the river's cur-rent, the deckhand on the *Fearless* had pulled the two stern holding pins that held the towline in place at the centre of the stern. The towline, a greased steel cable four inches thick, veered wildly from side to side, scraping across the tug's stern steel bumper, while the deckhand cowered behind the winch.

AMONG THOSE ON deck watching the slow progress of the tug and barge were Stanley Shanks and Karl Pedersen. The fat man was keeping close to Shanks, trying to contain the little chainsaw salesman's panic, so his knowledge of Pedersen's swindle wouldn't spread throughout the ship.

Stanley had not sold a single chainsaw and in an attempt to recoup his losses, he had invested the remainder of his wife's money in Pedersen's mining stock.

"Get in on the ground floor," Pedersen had told Shanks when he took the bait.

But now, it seemed, there was also a basement.

"Couldn't you just give me my money back?"

"Afraid not. Since this recent downturn the stock is no longer worth what you paid for it, so I'd be out of pocket."

But it was Shanks who was out of pocket. He had, in fact, written a cheque to Pedersen for his wife's entire inheritance, confident, as Pedersen had assured him, that in a matter of weeks he would double his money.

"What am I to do?"

"Best thing is to just wait it out. In for a dime, in for a dollar, I always say. Of course," said the fat man, "you could easily turn this situation to your advantage."

"How so?"

"Don't you see?" asked Pederson. "With prices rock bottom like this you should buy up all the stock you can get your hands on."

Shanks looked at the fat man as if he were mad.

"Look," said Pedersen, "We're turning around."

The *Cardena* was indeed coming about and heading downstream.

"Just have to hang on, ride it out," advised Pedersen.

Shanks gripped the rail. He thought he might throw up. Where would he get the money to pay the Swedes' wages and how would he control them when they found out he was broke?

THE *CARDENA* MADE her way downstream on the Skeena, stopping on the north side of the river to take on more salmon. Here, in the heart of the northern salmon fishery, the ship called at cannery after cannery, Haysport, then on to Inverness Passage: Cassiar, Sunnyside, North Pacific, and Inverness.

In the canneries the generators ran through the night. Indian women sloshed around in fish slime as they washed, packed, and cooked salmon. All night long the *Cardena*'s winches hissed and reeled pallets piled with cases of canned salmon into its holds. There was no time for sleep.

Boyce counted the rungs of the ladder from the dock to the water. The tide was dropping and the ship's draught was increasing as the load got heavier. It was time to get out before they hit bottom.

"Shut the door, will you?"

Briggs had come into the wheelhouse, the rank smell of the cannery wafting in with him. He had been working below deck for eighteen hours straight, loading salmon cases, and now he was due to stand watch at the wheel for six hours.

Boyce looked at Briggs, who could hardly stand. Nothing was more hypnotic and sleep inducing than standing watch in the darkness of the wheelhouse.

"Grab some shut-eye and I'll take us out," Boyce said.

It was the least he could do. They would make the tide and he hadn't run aground. They had only to unload cargo at Prince Rupert and call at the Nass River canneries. After the Nass, it was a quick run up Observatory Inlet to Anyox, and then the beginning of the return trip south.

It had been a good trip but he couldn't stop worrying about the boy. He felt responsible. He would give himself a few days, and then, if he was still worried about Matt, Boyce knew what he'd do, even if it meant putting the schedule in jeopardy.

XX

AS THE *CARDENA* STEAMED UP Observatory Inlet toward Anyox, the knowledge of their inevitable and final separation closed in on Monica and Cameron like the canyon walls on either side of their ship.

Every gesture, every remark was tempered by this knowledge. Whether they were prepared to admit it or not, each of them was already withdrawing from the other as a kind of self defence. Gone was the openness and freedom they had felt earlier on the voyage, when time seemed to stop. Now they were running out of time.

It would be over soon enough. All Monica wanted now was for it to end, to be at the mine. She wished she'd never laid eyes on Cameron. It was too painful.

In the meantime she attempted to cope by locking herself in her cabin where she read and drank. She didn't care what she read as long as the pages filled her time. There was a small library in the lounge where she had found a copy of Martha Ostenso's *Wild Geese* and a few mysteries, but she had long since exhausted its meagre offerings and was now reduced to reading a Union Steamship promotional booklet titled *Our Coastal Trips*.

Fourteen steamships were listed on the title page, the *Cardena*, the flagship of the fleet, at the top. She turned the page, lit a

Gitane, inhaled, and blew the smoke onto a page of exaggerated promotional copy: "The trip from Vancouver to Prince Rupert and the North is both interesting and delightful . . . a never-ending kaleidoscope of marine and mountain scenery . . . ," the pages flipping by in a blur of superlatives and hyperbole until she reached the last page of the booklet, the end of her journey, her destination.

> But now the passenger is being hastened forward to one
> of the greatest mining centres in the world—Anyox,
> a mining town of the Granby Mining, Smelting and
> Power Co., Ltd.
>
> Anyox, with a population of two thousand, is
> situated on Observatory Inlet, ninety miles north of
> Prince Rupert. This copper mine and smelter has been
> enormously developed during recent years, until it now
> ranks as the largest copper mine in the British Empire.

She couldn't believe her good fortune. She had only to sober up and make herself presentable when Jenkins met her on the dock.

She kept repeating the phrase to herself, "The largest mine in the British Empire." Her fingers closed on a glass and she raised it to her lips. "Here's to the largest mine in the British Empire."

There was a loud rap on the door of her cabin. She walked toward it, steadying herself. "Who is it?"

"Cameron. It's me, Cameron."

"What do you want?"

"We're almost there."

"Yes, but where?"

"Anyox, the copper mine. Where you're getting off," he said, choking on the words. "You'd better hurry. We're about to dock."

"But I'm not ready."

"I'll help you." But the truth was he couldn't help himself. He couldn't stay away. Cameron was locked in a kind of helpless doom. He had turned that around once when they were supposed to have parted at Port Hardy and he had remained aboard the *Cardena*, but now he had to face their final parting.

Halfway down the gangplank Monica almost lost her footing.

"Easy," said Cameron and hooked his arm under hers.

FROM THE *CARDENA*'S bridge Wilson and Boyce watched the couple on the dock. "I don't know why that woman wanted off here," said Wilson. "I hate this place. We sail all the way up the Inside Passage and what do we find at the northern end of our journey?"

"Anyox," answered Boyce.

"A man-made little hellhole seventeen kilometres from the border between Alaska and British Columbia."

"Not so little," countered Boyce. "And I like the dock. It's a proper dock, not like the rickety little wharves we tie up to. There's room for four ocean-going freighters on this dock."

THE DOCK STRETCHED around the waterfront like a giant veranda. Ore cars clanked along the rail line that ran from the mine to the smelter, while overhead cranes carried coal from the dock to the coke plant where it was turned into hot fuel for the smelter.

There was no one on the dock to greet Monica and this seemed odd to her. Cameron set Monica's suitcases down and they walked to the company offices. Even though it was evening and well past business hours, Monica rapped loudly on the office door.

"Closed," called a voice from behind them. "This is a company town. The whole town is private property and you two are trespassing. I'm the night watchman. What are you doing here?"

Monica and Cameron turned to face a frail elderly man.

"I'm here to visit Stuart Jenkins, the mine manager," Monica said. "Please inform him Monica James has arrived."

"Jenkins? There's no Stuart Jenkins here. Had a Stuart Jenkins who was a foreman, not a mine manager, but he cleared out more than a month ago."

"Why did he leave?" asked Monica.

"Same reason anyone leaves, for their health. See those trees on the hillside?"

In the lights from the town the trees looked like silver-grey skeletons. "Dead. All the vegetation between here and Alice Arm's been killed by sulfur fumes from the smelter."

"If that's what the fumes have done to the trees, just think what those fumes are doing to the lungs of the men who work in the smelter," said Cameron.

"We call the smelter workers 'gas eaters.' After two hours in the smelter they start spitting up yellow phlegm. Four years ago we were fog-bound for two weeks and the fog trapped the gas at ground level. We all got nosebleeds. Stuffed newspapers around doors and windows to try to keep the gas out but there's no escaping it, not in Anyox."

The night sky flared a fiery red, momentarily casting its light on the faces of the old man, Monica, and Cameron. "They're bringing the coke out of the furnaces—fuel for the smelter that produces the copper and that goddamn gas."

JENKINS HAD TOLD her in his letters he would be here, waiting for her. He wasn't manager of the mine, just a foreman. Monica felt betrayed and, worse, ashamed for what she had put Cameron through, and yet—what was happening to her?—it was as if a great weight was being lifted from her and she was filled with a sudden sense of relief. She had travelled to the far western edge of the continent where she had run out of land and run out of options. She had come to the end. She had dropped off the edge. She could die here. Right here, in this wasteland.

But there was a man here. A man who would not use her, who had seen her at her very worst and still accepted her, still wanted her. She had come to the end, to the edge, and she would go back, but she would go back with Cameron. She was sober now. She knew she had been drinking out of guilt for what she had done to him.

"We'd better get back," said Cameron. "Boyce won't wait for us. Not this time. Remember Campbell River? The only reason he brought the ship back to the dock was for Matthew."

"Yes," Monica replied. "He seemed so lost but then he found his father, so the trip turned out to be a wonderful success for him."

Cameron thought he sensed bitterness in her voice. As they bent to pick up her bags she turned and took a last look at the wasteland of dead trees and the fumes pouring out of the smelter's smokestack.

"You couldn't grow your garden here, Cameron."

They did not talk about themselves, about whether they had a future as a couple. It was too early for that.

"No," replied Cameron. "Not here."

XXI

THE *CARDENA* WAS HOMEWARD BOUND with eleven thousand forty-eight-pound cases of canned salmon in its hold, the crew already anticipating a day's shore leave in Vancouver. It was a good ship, a happy ship. Boyce liked the instant manoeuvrability the *Cardena*'s twin screws gave him at the canneries. It was just like working two oars in a rowboat . . . a rowboat . . . a goddamn rowboat. He had put that kid off his ship in the middle of the night in a rowboat with a man like Frank Clayton. Anything might happen. Boyce wouldn't rest until he saw the boy with his father. He would call in on the trip down. He wanted to know if Mac had been right or wrong in wanting to slide by with Matt asleep. He'd stop at Clayton's log raft and see for himself. Schedule be damned.

The mystery of the water: boiling white, rips, whirlpools, eddies, tidal streams scudding around hidden reefs, barriers. He had spent years on the Inside Passage; it was always different and it was always the same. On each voyage the same route south was followed: through Grenville Channel, across Queen Charlotte Sound to Port Hardy, Sointula, and Alert Bay, down Johnstone Strait, through Seymour Narrows, across the Gulf of Georgia, arriving in Vancouver Thursday afternoon and after only a day's layover, sailing north again Friday night, the same route repeated in reverse. "North By West In

The Sunlight" claimed the Union Steamship Company logo, but the *Cardena* left Vancouver late at night and the weather was not always fair.

"Where are we now, sir?" asked Briggs, pulling the old man out of his thoughts.

Boyce had forgotten this was his quartermaster's first trip. "Finlayson Channel. Those rocks you see up ahead in the middle of the channel, that's Sparrowhawk Reef."

"A pretty name."

"Maybe so, but you want to steer clear of those rocks. They're named after a British light naval cruiser that went aground there in 1874, the *Sparrowhawk*."

He didn't tell Briggs that the *Catala*, under his command, had been impaled on those same rocks. It would be like that all the way down the coast. The *Cardena* would pass a certain point of land or go through a particular body of water, and he would be reminded of other passages in that same water.

Morning found Briggs and Boyce ready to begin their six o'clock watch and take the *Cardena* across Queen Charlotte Sound to the northern tip of Vancouver Island. White clouds lifting above Bilton Island, scarcely a ripple on the water, the promise of a smooth crossing, a promise that had been broken many times by the forty miles of open sea that lay ahead of them.

And why was he remembering all this now, on the beautiful calm day of a perfect crossing? Because the return trip south was a time for remembrances and reminiscing. Was he just being sentimental in his old age or was it because he sensed that the time of the Union ships and the isolated communities they served was already passing?

Having given his quartermaster a course to steer by, Boyce stepped out of the wheelhouse to water his plants. On the clear September day the brisk sea air was intoxicating. It made him giddy, glad to be alive. He bent with his watering can over his little planter box. A plant that a woman up the coast had given him was just now showing a single bloom. It had the same configuration as a common daisy but was larger, the colours more intriguing, the petals a wine colour, becoming brown, and at the centre, a yellow as bright as the sun.

A SPECK ON the horizon trailing a thread of black smoke into a blue sky, the *Cardena* steamed across Queen Charlotte Sound toward Port Hardy while Emily waited on the dock.

On her journey to the centre of Vancouver Island, something had revealed itself to her in the Indian village on Quatsino Sound: a huge carved figure with an open mouth and a two-headed sea serpent carved across its head—D'Sonoqua, the mythical wild woman of the woods.

XXII

"SURE YOU DON'T WANT US to go in with you, skipper?" Springline called down to Boyce, who was in the lifeboat Springline and Soogie Phelps were lowering from the *Cardena*.

"I'll go alone," Boyce called up to his deckhands.

Fearing the worst—whatever he might find at Clayton's camp—he didn't want his crew to see, for he felt he had let them down by allowing Matt to leave the *Cardena*. He undid the ropes, pushed the lifeboat free, and began rowing to shore.

"Don't come no closer. I'll shoot!"

Oars stilled just above the water's surface, Boyce let the lifeboat glide forward. He had seen men like this. Couldn't stand the loneliness, the isolation, ended up shooting at trees. Bushed. This one he couldn't even see, just a voice in the trees. Boyce's boat was within range of a madman's rifle.

"Where's the boy?"

"Cleared out. Stole my boat. Rowed out in the middle of the night. Well, he won't get far. And what am I supposed to do? I'm stranded here. Can't get out without a boat."

Boyce spun the lifeboat around and began rowing back to the *Cardena*. "Get the Indians to help you!" he shouted, pulling on the oars.

The boy was probably dead now, drowned in that little tub his father called a boat. Boyce had no one to blame but himself. If he'd kept on going that night and not left Matt with his father, the boy would still be alive. Boyce rowed furiously back to his ship, wondering what the father had done to drive Matt off after the boy had come all this way.

XXIII

THE TREES MATT'S FATHER WAS falling into the sea were central to the Kwakiutl way of life. Cedar was the substance, the medium, the material on which their culture was built, the miracle tree that clothed and sheltered the people. The night Matt's rowboat was pulled by the boys up onto the beach, he was too involved with his immediate survival to see that the women digging clams wore skirts and shawls woven from the soft, shredded bark of the cedar tree.

The boys were like guardians protecting him. They were proud of their discovery and wouldn't let him out of their sight, and this gave Matt some sense of security. They had found a white boy washed up on the shore in the bottom of a boat. For the boys, and the people of the village, the event was almost mythic.

The Kwakiutl addressed the spirit of the western red cedar as "Long Life Maker" and used every part of the tree. The withes, slender branchlets that hang down from the main branches of the tree in long, graceful curves, were used to make rope and the burden baskets the women placed their clams in. When the sap ran in spring and early summer, women stripped bark from standing cedar trees to weave blankets, shawls, skirts, mats, hats.

The boys had been delegated to split planks and had enlisted Matt as their helper. On the beach they marked a line across the butt of a long, straight-grain cedar log and along this line hammered in six yew wedges. As the wedges were driven farther into the log, each blow of the hammer was accompanied by a cracking sound; the fibres of the wood let go and split apart a few more inches.

Each time the log made this cracking sound, the boys stopped hammering and looked at each other as if they were listening to the sound of the soul or the heart of the wood coming asunder, and as it did so it released the cedar's pungent, citrus-like scent. When the cracking sound subsided, the boys resumed their hammering and, when they were unable to drive the wedges in any farther from the end, they began to drive them in along the length of the log until at last the crack opened, splitting the log in half lengthwise.

Now they had two flat surfaces from which they could split out the actual planks, using the same procedure repeated at one-inch intervals down the base of each half of the log. Each time the board sprang free from the wedges, Matt was amazed to see the miracle of the cedar reveal itself in its most elemental form: straight, one-inch-thick, three-foot-wide boards twelve feet long, made without the use of a sawmill.

The boys took a brief break from their labour, and Matt joined them where they sat on half of the split log on the beach, facing the sea, the village houses behind them. The smell of alder smoke drifted up through sides of salmon and out through the cedar-plank roof of the smokehouse, reaching the boys on the beach. One of them left and returned minutes later with some salmon, the flesh dried a deep maroon colour.

They sat on the log, chewing the sweet, dry salmon in silence, staring out at the wind-wrinkled blue water. Was this not the perfect life? thought Matt. And yet, more than when he had walked onto the reserve at Alert Bay, Matt felt like an outsider, a curiosity. He was a boy, fifteen years old, lost in a strange and alien world, safe for the moment but for how long he didn't know.

Most of the men of the village were fishing or working in the canneries and the boys had been left in the care of the women. They could not speak English and Matthew was trying to communicate with them in the only way he knew how, very carefully, with a stick, outlining a shape in the sand.

He wanted to make his image of the *Cardena* big, so there would be no mistaking it for another ship. He got up and walked the length of the log, tracing the hull in the sand, while the two boys sat and watched. He added the cabin and, above it a funnel, a crude cloud of smoke billowing out of it, and even though he was unsure whether they could read it, he neatly lettered the name on the bow, *Cardena*.

The boys began talking excitedly among themselves. That very spring the *Cardena* had brought to their village a missionary who had persuaded the elders to enroll the boys in Saint Michael's Indian Residential School in Alert Bay. They were now in the final days of their freedom. Tomorrow they would go across the water to Alert Bay where they knew the *Cardena* always stopped, and they would take Matt along with them.

THEY HAD TO cross open water to get to Alert Bay, so they would be accompanied by one of the women who had been clamming on the beach the night they discovered Matt.

Their craft was a dugout canoe, the sides forced outward by steam, gunwales gracefully lifting at the bow and stern. They carried it to the water on fir poles padded with cedar bark and set it down tenderly at the edge of the sea as if it were a living thing. Painted on its side, the ovoid eye of some strange sea creature stared at Matt. A carved cedar raven's beak thrust out over the bow. Perhaps the canoe *was* a living thing.

He watched it float and bob in perfect balance without ballast, the movement of the raven's beak reflected in the water. Maybe all vessels were living things. He thought of the *Cardena* in this way. In the *Cardena* he had been at sea; now, in this impossibly small canoe, he would be *in* the sea, his baptism in the morning calm of the sheltered bay, water lapping gently against the canoe as an old man shoved them from the shore. They slid effortlessly through the green sea: the woman at the helm, followed by her boys, then Matt, blades poised at shoulder height, thrust in sudden unison into the sea, raised, repeated, over and over, the way the boys had shown Matt.

AN AFTERNOON WIND rippled across the surface and found the canoe. The boys steadied the dugout while the woman kept them on course, heading into the wind. An hour later it had turned into a gale that tossed the canoe into the air like the light, hollowed-out piece of wood it was, then slammed it down into the churning sea.

Matt couldn't believe this was happening to him. Was this his punishment for abandoning his father? The beak of the great bird at the prow of their craft probed the wall of sea that rose before them.

Who, after all, had abandoned whom? It didn't matter now. All that mattered was his survival. He thrust his paddle into the seething sea and joined in the shouts and yells of the two boys bracing themselves for the onslaught of the next wave.

XXIV

ON THE SOUTHBOUND ROUTE, AT the port of call just before
Alert Bay, the *Cardena* loomed larger as Koko paced the far end of
the dock and barked at the ship drawing closer to Port Hardy.

Then the *Cardena* steamed toward Alert Bay with Emily
onboard. When Boyce went off watch he would ask her about her
trip to Quatsino, whether she had found what she was looking for.
Over the years he had watched and worried over her solitary journeys. He had heard that thirty years before, on one of the smaller
boats that plied the outside run to Ucluelet, the ship's purser had
fallen in love with Emily and then followed her to London where
she was studying art.

He was wondering about this when the first mate, Grayson,
came into the wheelhouse. "Cameron and Monica James want to
speak with you, sir."

What could they possibly want from him now? Of course, they
wanted him to marry them. He would refuse, not outright, but tell
them he couldn't, wasn't qualified. They weren't in international
waters and he didn't have deep sea papers.

"I'll meet them in the officers' mess when I come off watch at
noon." He didn't want that woman in the wheelhouse ever again.

"Right," said Grayson.

My God. The things you had to do. When Grayson had left the wheelhouse Boyce said to Briggs, "Did I ever tell you about the time a baby was born aboard ship?"

Briggs always felt privileged when Boyce broke the long periods of silence of their standing watch together, but out of respect for the old man, he seldom initiated a conversation unless it was strictly a matter regarding bearings. "No, sir, you didn't."

"That was an experience for you, boy! If it hadn't been for the chief steward, I think that baby would have died. The freight clerks were asleep in the cabin ahead of this young fellow and his wife. She was about nineteen, I guess. He wasn't much older. When the pain started, she screamed like bloody murder and the two freight clerks took off. They didn't know what was happening. The chief steward came up to me and said, 'We've got a birth coming.'

"I said, 'Oh, no. Don't say that. She can't last out, eh?'

"'No.'

"'We'd better get the book out,' I said.

"We got the book out, trying to read all about it, you know. You ever try to read a book with the sweat coming down your face and the woman screaming her head off? We wanted the husband to do something. We turned around and he had fainted right there.

"'We'll have to get lots of hot water, Captain,' said the steward.

"I said, 'Turn the whole bloody crew out, we got an emergency. Who knows, someone may have done this before.' But nobody wanted any part of it.

"But we did it and we got her to Rupert all right. None of us were quite sure of that cord. The book just said cut the cord. It didn't say cut it here or anywhere. Where the hell do you cut it?

Anyhow, we cut it pretty close and we got her into Rupert. That was out of my line, completely. That was a frightening experience. The baby was doing fine, but you only want that to happen once in your life if you're not a doctor. I'd rather go up the Skeena in a snowstorm than go through that again."

Boyce rang for Slow Ahead, and the *Cardena* entered Alert Bay. He always looked forward to stopping there but not today, when he knew he would be meeting with Cameron and Monica as soon as he'd docked his ship.

XXV

FROM WHERE THEY STOOD ON deck Stanley Shanks and Karl Pedersen watched a dugout canoe coming toward the *Cardena*.

"Indians," said Pedersen. "They sell things to the tourists."

But as the canoe came closer they saw that the boy in the middle was not Indian. From the upper deck Springline recognized Matt first.

"The boy is coming aboard! It's Matt! He's come back!" Word passed among the crew until it seemed the ship itself chorused, "The boy is returning!"

Those words, shouted all over his ship, woke Boyce from the worst nightmare of his life, that he had been responsible for Matt's death. "The boy is returning!"

Monica and Cameron were there and Emily and Koko, and Springline, Boyce, the whole crew gathered around Matt on the forward deck. They all saw that Matt had changed. There was a roughness about his appearance. His clothes were ragged and torn, and there was a hardness in his face. What had happened? they wondered.

The initial jubilance of greetings subsided and a sudden hollowness descended on Matt. He broke from their embraces, rushed to the railing on the forward deck, and stared down into the dark waters of Alert Bay.

"What's the matter with Matt?" someone asked.

Below him, dwarfed by the height and bulk of the *Cardena*, the small cedar dugout with the two boys and the woman under the broad brim of a cedar-bark hat bumped against the ship's steel hull. They had waited to make sure Matt was safely onboard, and seeing him peer down at them over the *Cardena*'s railing, they waved up at him. From the deck Matt waved back at the boys to whom he owed his life. They were the only reason he was onboard the *Cardena*.

Oar blades set against the steel hull, the boys pushed off from the ship. They dipped their oars and the canoe cut through the water, now moving away from the *Cardena* and toward the school at the end of the bay. The woman in the canoe took off her hat and grey hair tumbled across her shoulders. Matt watched them paddle away. What will happen to them now, and how would the canoe get back to their village with only the old woman to paddle it? he wondered. Later, he saw the canoe tied to the pilings at Cook's Cannery. It bobbed on the afternoon chop as if it had a life of its own.

Matt's mother was dead and he had turned his back on his father, but he saw that in some way, he was part of a larger family. The old Indian woman, the boys, and everyone on the ship—Boyce, Springline, Mackinnon, Cameron, Monica, and Emily, even the ship itself. They had all embraced him and he must return that embrace. He turned from the railing toward the people waiting on deck to greet him.

XXVI

BOYCE SMELLED HER SCENT BEFORE he even opened the door to the officers' mess. Monica seemed oddly distracted, as if she weren't quite there, or perhaps couldn't believe where she really was. It occurred to Boyce that ever since Anyox, she had been coming apart. Her face was flushed and her long brown hair, which she normally wore down, was tied in a bun that was now coming undone in coils at her neck. She's been drinking, thought Boyce. Once she had been attractive, others thought her beautiful. Now she was going to hell and taking Cameron with her. He hated her for that.

Cameron did the talking. He didn't seem to notice Monica's condition. He was holding her hand, as if in reassurance. "We have a favour to ask of you."

"Yes?" Here it comes, Boyce thought. He had already prepared his answer.

"When the *Cardena* leaves Alert Bay, could you take the ship around the north end of Cormorant Island, instead of the south end, like you usually do?"

"I suppose, but . . ." This wasn't what he'd expected at all. Still, Cormorant was a small island and a minor course alteration wouldn't put him out much. But it just didn't make sense. "Why?"

"There's another island off Cormorant and I've purchased a piece of land there."

"Yes?" Boyce still didn't understand.

"We, Monica and I, we're wondering if you could set us off there. You see, we're going to build a house."

"The two of you are going to build a house on raw land, in the forest, on an island?"

The woman, he knew, hadn't the slightest idea where she was and seemed to be doing her best to maintain that state.

"Not just the two of us," replied Cameron. "We're hoping to hire Matt for the rest of the fall."

"What you're doing is mad but you can't involve the boy. He's just gotten back onboard the ship."

"In case you haven't noticed, Captain Boyce, Matthew doesn't quite seem a boy anymore, and anyhow, it's what he wants. He told us so."

This, from the woman. Boyce couldn't believe his ears. He opened the door and called out to Grayson, "Get the boy, Matt, that is, Matthew Clayton, in here right now." He closed the door and turned to Monica and Cameron. "I want to hear what Matt has to say."

They waited in awkward silence. Boyce had become entangled in the lives of his passengers, something he always tried to avoid. He took some comfort in the thought that if they got off his ship, he would be rid of them.

There was a knock on the varnished wood door of the officers' mess and Matt stepped inside.

"Is this true?" asked Boyce.

The truth was Monica and Cameron were Matt's friends and they had asked him. The truth was he couldn't face the crew. They had set him off in the middle of the night with his father. Matt had found his father but it had all gone wrong and now here he was back on the *Cardena*. They'd want to know what had happened and Matt was having trouble sorting it out for himself. He was ashamed, embarrassed, couldn't face them. Better to go with Cameron and Monica than stay on the *Cardena*, because in a few days, the ship would end up back in Vancouver. What could he possibly do in that city, so different from the island he had grown up on? The island now idealized in his memory, where he and his mother and father had lived together as a family.

Matt was running away again; he had been running since the night he made off in his father's rowboat, running away from the truth. This was the story he told himself: he hadn't planned to leave his father; he had just needed to get away for a while, row off some anger, but he rowed too far and got lost. But the truth was he'd wanted to get away from his father. He'd run out on his own father and left him stranded without a boat.

"Well son, speak up now," said Boyce.

"Just for the rest of the fall, until winter sets in. Until we get the roof on."

Boyce noticed the authoritative tone in Matt's use of the word "we." The woman was right. Not the language of a boy, not at all.

Still, it was insane. Cameron had apparently lost his mind. He could refuse, of course. By the time he set them off in a lifeboat, then waited for his deckhand to row back to the *Cardena*, he'd be an hour behind schedule. And yet, in the end, what business was it of his? People came and went on his ship, and once they were off it, well, goodbye.

"All right, then. I suppose we can manage it, but I can't leave the lifeboat with you." A simple enough statement, the lifeboat had to return to the *Cardena*, but Boyce intended to emphasize the extreme isolation they would face without even a boat. "You understand?"

"Of course," said Cameron.

"Right, then." Cameron, Monica, and Matt were leaving the officers' mess when Boyce blurted, "No, wait! This isn't right!"

Cameron turned to confront the captain. "Isn't right? What do you mean, it isn't right?"

"Isn't right," Boyce stammered, "without a boat. We'll break out that little punt back of the upper cabins."

Boyce felt as if he were throwing a drowning man a life raft but that the man was going to drown anyway.

"WHAT'S HAPPENING?" ASKED Stanley.

The deckhands were removing the canvas cover from a lifeboat. "Lifeboat drill, I expect," said Pedersen.

But Matt, Monica, Cameron, and Springline were climbing into the lifeboat and it was being swung out from the deck and lowered over the side on its davits. Monica seemed lost in thought, arriving at a destination she had never planned.

"By God," said Pedersen, "they're putting those people ashore."

"But there's nothing there, nothing but trees."

Passengers and crew watched in silent vigil as the lifeboat, towing a small punt filled with Cameron's tools, and Monica's and

Matt's bags, made its way from the *Cardena* to the small island in the distance.

EMILY AND BOYCE watched the three of them stand on the shore, a narrow margin of smooth, round rocks between the sea and the forest that rose like a green curtain behind them. Boyce trained his binoculars on the island. Giant Sitka spruce and old-growth cedar grew right down to the shore, stopped by the high-water mark, but not completely, for in seeking the sunlight at the edge of the forest, their branches angled over the sea. Trees grew to the very edge, where at high tide, waves washed and tumbled stones against the trunks of the giant shore dwellers. The action of the stones wore away the bark and the trees bled a translucent amber sap that hardened in the sun on the bare, exposed, white sapwood.

What happened to people? Boyce wondered. Something got hold of them and wouldn't let go, an obsession, something out of control. Blind, he thought, blind instinct.

Quite suddenly, Monica, Matt, and Cameron stepped through the curtain of trees and disappeared.

Springline was already rowing the lifeboat back to the *Cardena*. Boyce rang for Stand By. He would make up the lost hour somehow, and at least Cameron and Monica were off his ship.

But Boyce couldn't let it go. He told himself it was because of Matt. He felt responsible. On the following week's run he altered his course. It was a small thing—he simply took the *Cardena* around the other side of Cormorant Island—but he kept to his new course thereafter, each week passing as close to the small island as he dared take the *Cardena*, searching the beach and the forest beyond for signs of human life: fire, blue smoke drifting up through the tree-tops. But there was nothing. He half expected one of them, the woman, the boy, perhaps even Cameron, to be hailing him from the shore, wanting out in defeat, but no, there was no sign of them. Still, he took to blowing the *Cardena*'s whistle as he passed, just to let them know he was there if, in fact, they heard it. If, Boyce worried, they were still alive.

XXVII

A MONTH WENT BY AND a small landing raft appeared offshore, and then, on the following week's passage, Matt stood on the raft, hailing the *Cardena*. While he waited, he had been jigging for cod from the raft. They had been living off clams, mussels, and, at low tide, crab caught in the eelgrass.

Yes, Matt told Springline, everything was going well. He and Cameron had succeeded in falling some trees and cutting them into pole lengths. Monica had peeled the poles using a drawknife. Boyce tried to envision the worldly Monica James straddling a log and pulling a drawknife, but he couldn't. The final poles had not peeled easily because the sap had stopped running, and the three were afraid of the weather closing in on them before the roof was on.

Matt told Springline he would stay until they had completed the building, or at least the roof. Springline presented Boyce with a long list of supplies they needed, tools, bitts, huge bolts to join the timbers to the poles, and steel expansion rings to take the weight of the timbers. He put the list and an envelope of cash in the same jacket pocket in which he had placed so many forgotten scraps of paper, then thought better of it and gave the list and the money to his purser.

Sometime in November, Boyce saw a small clearing and a number of peeled poles braced upright. Matt, Monica, and Cameron were working night and day to close the place in before winter. Though the wedges and hammers they used were a newer design, they made cedar planks in the age-old manner the two Kwakiutl boys had employed. Without a sawmill, they had no choice.

Cameron's guiding philosophy was to use the materials at hand, and so the thing grew, it seemed, out of the land, a great bird feathered in cedar planks and shakes, sitting on poles joined together with rough adzed timbers in classic pole frame design modelled after the old man's house in Kelsey Bay.

ALMOST TWO MONTHS later, they were unloading supplies onto the landing raft: tools, chickens in crates, and a goat. As usual, only Matt was present. Where were Cameron and Monica? Boyce was looking over the rail. Had they become so bushed that they now shunned all contact with the outside world?

"Cameron and Monica would like you to join us for a late lunch!" Matt shouted from the landing raft.

There would be hell to pay with the schedule. He would lose an hour while the whole crew sat and waited, but his curiosity had got the better of him.

They were living in the house and still building it. It occurred to Boyce that they would be building it forever, an organic thing that would grow with them. The main floor was an open space with no rooms, the kitchen at one end, the living room at the other, and in the centre, fashioned out of a huge steel oil drum, a wood stove. They had no bricks to line it with so they had filled the bottom with sand from the beach.

Like the main floor, the second floor was an open design entirely given over to a bedroom. Matt was sleeping on a makeshift cot near the kitchen on the main floor.

Presiding over all this was a woman who had travelled the world and at last had found her home, a woman unlike any Boyce had ever seen, certainly not the woman who had been onboard the *Cardena*. It was the same woman, and yet, it was as if Boyce were seeing her for the first time, the woman Cameron had seen all along. Cameron had grown a beard and moved more slowly, with an unhurried peace and containment, secure in the knowledge that for himself and Monica, there would always be a tomorrow.

All around them towered huge trees, growing so close their branches brushed the sides of the house when the wind blew.

"Aren't you afraid these big trees might fall on the house during a wind storm?"

"Yes. There's always that risk, but here's the thing. If we cut down the trees, then we create a path for the wind to blow down more trees. So it's best to just live with them."

They were enclosed in the forest, and Boyce remembered, watching from the deck of the *Cardena*, that moment when they had first vanished.

They sat around a long cedar-slab table and Monica served a chowder of steamed clams, crabs, and mussels. "The clams are so plentiful you don't have to dig them, just rake the surface sand with a stick," she said.

The chowder was followed by a fillet of spring salmon steamed on a cedar plank. It separated into moist flakes at the touch of Boyce's fork.

"There are so many salmon you can catch them casting from the shore," said Matt.

They were drinking something made from salal berries. It wasn't wine, but it seemed to have alcohol in it.

"You know, Captain Boyce, we will always be thankful for the way you treated us. You quite literally altered your course to include us."

"It was nothing," he said, embarrassed to hear this gratitude from a woman who, when she had been onboard his ship, he had despised. "Nothing at all," he repeated.

"Oh, but it was," she insisted. "And now we have one more favour to ask of you."

"Yes?"

"Matt's work here with us is finished and much as we would like him to stay, he feels it is time to leave. Could you take him on the *Cardena*?"

"Of course," he said, feeling the effects of the salal drink. "Passengers and freight. That's the *Cardena*."

"No. That's not what we mean at all. Could you take him on as crew?"

"He's a little young, don't you think?"

"But you sent him up the mast."

"That was my first mate's idea."

"I *was* a day man," interrupted Matt.

"A day man. Chipping and painting. That's very different from shift work, six on, six off, twelve hours a day, and that's just for starters. A deckhand's on call every port we make, manhandling lines and freight. Those men on the Skeena worked thirty-six hours straight." He turned to Monica. "You saw it. You were there.

I tell you, it's too much for a fifteen-year-old boy."

"It wasn't too much for him to help build this house," Cameron broke in.

"Yes," said Monica. "He's young. And that's just why we can't let him go into the world alone. Don't you see? The *Cardena's* perfect. It's where he belongs."

"I talked it over with Springline," explained Matt. "When I was waiting on our landing raft. He's promised to show me the ropes."

"All right, then, son." Boyce stood up from the table. "You can start by rowing me back to the *Cardena*."

"Yessir!"

They were almost like a family as they walked together to the water's edge. Cameron and Monica stood together on the shore and watched as the lifeboat bumped alongside the *Cardena*, and Boyce and Matt were hoisted aboard.

"What are you thinking?"

"We never would have met if it hadn't been for that ship."

"It's a good ship. Matt will do just fine."

They turned then and re-entered the forest.

From the *Cardena* Matt looked for them but they were already gone. And yet he knew they were there, hidden in the trees. They would always be there.

XXVIII

IN THE BARS AND ALONG the waterfront, sailors with no vessel to ship out on wandered, landlocked, searching for memories of their lost ships. They gathered at reunions and they brought and exchanged photos and mementoes and stories of the Union ships they had sailed on.

Matt attended a reunion aboard the *Lady Alexandra*. She had been turned into a floating restaurant anchored in Vancouver's harbour. The ship never left its moorings and the meals were expensive, but not, the men agreed, as good as Union fare.

They met for the camaraderie of being with their old shipmates and they talked of the final fate of each Union ship as if they were talking about their own fate, and they were, for the ships and the men had been inseparable. Matt listened, anxious to hear the final resting place of the *Cardena*; he had served on her until the company folded in 1958.

He did not study and write for his tickets and become a mate or a captain, but instead, he was a quartermaster. He had his own cabin, and from the day he first stepped onboard the *Cardena* as a boy, the wheelhouse had always been his favourite part of the ship. For twenty-eight years he stood watch, steering the *Cardena*. Now he had come to the reunion to find out where she was.

He listened to a skipper recall the last days of the *Cassiar* as if he and the ship were one and the same. "I was the last ship in. I came in with the *Cassiar* with one hundred and twenty-five tons of frozen fish and there wasn't a bloody soul to tell me what to do with it. Not a soul. 'Do you know where they want the fish, George?' The policeman on the dock said, 'There's nobody here, Captain, and they don't tell us nothing. I don't even think they know you're out.' 'Well, I'm not out now, I'm in. But what the hell am I going to do with a hundred and twenty-five tons of bloody frozen halibut?' Well, the only thing I could do was tell the engineer he would have to run the freezer all night. Imagine, not a bloody soul was there.

"It was in the hands of vultures. What they were after was Bowen Island, which Union Steamship owned. They didn't want the company's ships but they had to take them if they took the island. That's all there was to it."

"My God, I thought, this is the end," said an oiler who had signed on to the *Venture* for her last voyage. She had been sold to the Chinese, renamed the *Hsin Kong So*, and was sailing for Shanghai. "When I went aboard her and stepped down into the engine room, everything was leaking and blowing steam. You needed an umbrella just to walk around."

The *Hsin Kong So* completed the first leg of her journey across the Pacific, arriving in Hawaii only to be completely gutted by fire at dockside in Honolulu.

The oiler passed around the table a photograph of the ship that had served the coastal communities of BC for thirty-five years. "Hell, man. She caught fire so fast I couldn't even get my stuff off. I was running around on the dock in my underwear!"

Springline held the photo in his hands and stared in disbelief at the lopsided ship, ravaged by fire, leaning into Pier 7 E. "It's lucky you were in Hawaii and not Canada. You'd have froze your balls off."

Springline had been drinking. Matt leaned across the table, trying to get the attention of his old shipmate who, he knew, had lived onboard until the end.

"And the *Cardena*? What happened to the *Cardena*? Where is she now?"

"They towed her to Victoria and tore her apart for scrap. You'd think that was enough, wouldn't you? But no. They weren't finished with her yet. When they'd taken everything off her and there was nothing left but the hull, they towed her up the coast and used her for a breakwater."

The frail man who had been gassed in the war, and on whom Boyce had relied every day to handle lines on the ship they had called the lifeline of the coast, sat across from Matt, sobbing.

XXIX

SOME TWENTY MILES OUTSIDE VANCOUVER the Trans-Canada Highway unwinds out of the cliffs and ends at the western edge of the continent where miles of cars with nowhere left to go crawl down the side of a hill and disappear into the black hole of a ship's hold.

A NEW DEPARTURE EVERY HOUR ON THE HOUR

"What will we do with Dad?" the woman asked her husband as he turned off the ignition in their luxury SUV. It had become a recurring question that they thought they had answered by placing him in the Sunnyside Seniors Rest Home, but when the old man heard they were taking their kids to Vancouver Island for a few days, he had insisted on coming. It was a question they knew they would be asking themselves many times on this trip.

Behind them their two children fidgeted and squirmed, anxious to get out and explore the ship. The old man dozed fitfully.

"We could just leave him here in the car while we take the kids above deck," he offered. "It's less than two hours to the other side." But he knew it was a bad idea.

"Suppose he wakes up while we're gone? He won't even know where he is. No, we either have to stay below in the car with him or wake him up and take him above deck with us."

The children suddenly ended this debate by yelling in their grandfather's ears. "Wake up, Gramps! We want to see the ship!"

Crammed into an elevator, the family ascended through three levels of decks. The doors opened, depositing them in the crowd on the passenger deck. Elbowing past youths lost in the electronic zap of video game screens, they stepped over a sill with the warning WATCH YOUR STEP, and stood behind a crate of life rafts that broke the brisk sea wind sweeping the empty outside deck. Gulls dropped from the railing to swoop over the green water, their wings touched by the spray of sea breaking into whitecaps. Matthew clutched the railing and watched a piece of driftwood toss in the chop. Beside him, his grandson stood on the second rung of the railing.

Matthew had still been half asleep in the elevator but now he had only to close his eyes and smell the sea to waken the memory of other voyages and to be again onboard the *Cardena*.

Over the years he had seen Monica and Cameron on trips they took to Vancouver for supplies. The couple had become recluses and seldom left their island. She had been a woman of the world but had become a woman of the coast. She wore men's pants and flannel shirts. She put on weight and her hair seemed to explode out of her head like a wild woman's, but Cameron loved her still.

They had bought a quarter horse and, on the journey back, she stayed with the small, frightened colt in steerage, feeding it alfalfa. "Except for Cameron, I prefer the company of animals," she had said to Matt, stroking the colt's mane.

She told Matt about the house he had helped them start, how she and Cameron had finished it, her garden. She asked Matt to visit but he never did. He seldom went ashore. Too many bad things had happened to him there. It was not the physical pain of his father throwing him down on the beach but the rejection of all he had sought that hurt and endured. He never went back and he never looked for his father again. He blamed himself. It was his fault he couldn't embrace his father as he was, not as he had wanted him to be.

Still, Cameron and Matt laughed when they remembered the day all three of them almost got stranded in Campbell River and Matt had his first taste of beer.

"Remember Shanks?" asked Cameron. "Whatever happened to him?"

"Never sold a single saw. Cost too much. No one could afford it. The depression, you know. And something else . . ." added Matt.

"Yes?"

"He never made it back to Vancouver."

"What do you mean?"

"When the *Cardena* docked in Vancouver, Shanks wasn't onboard. His wife was hysterical. All her money was gone and so was her husband. The police cordoned off the boat and wouldn't let anyone off until they'd interviewed the crew and passengers. Pedersen and the Swedes, Einar and Ollie, were all suspects, but the police couldn't prove anything and in the end it was ruled a suicide.

"I got all this from Boyce one night when we were standing watch together. We were going through Seymour Narrows and he said, 'This is where he must have jumped. Wouldn't stand a chance in that water.'"

When passengers came into the *Cardena*'s wheelhouse, they would see Matt standing at the wheel; when he was twenty-five, a young school teacher visited the wheelhouse and would not leave. They were married in the fall.

By then Boyce was the senior captain of the fleet and, like many Union captains, he died at sea aboard his ship. It was four days before Christmas and they were picking up some loggers in Menzies Bay when he collapsed on the bridge at the ship's telegraph. The first mate raced the ship back to the hospital at Campbell River with Matt at the wheel, but it was too late.

It was not, Matt reflected, a bad way to go, to die onboard your ship, but the *Cardena* had reached its end before him. Matt was eighty-five when the century turned and now he was going to find his ship again, for he knew where they had towed her last remains. In Victoria, Capital Iron and Metals had torn her apart, stripped her down to the hull for scrap, and then towed what remained of the hull to Kelsey Bay. He had known this ever since Springline told him at the reunion but couldn't bear to see her scrapped remains rusting away in that final resting place. Now he was going there. He wanted to see his ship one last time.

"HEY GRAMPS! SHIP'S docking. Time for us to go below."

With a start he realized they were almost on the other side of the strait. The entire crossing had taken little more than an hour. The passengers were already below deck, impatiently gunning their motors. The ship had no discernible bow or stern; the cars simply drove in one end and out the other. It was not so much a ship as a continuation of the highway, or a parking lot with an hour-and-three-quarters time limit, a long stoplight.

Cars streamed up the hill from the ferry slip out onto the highway, bumper-to-bumper traffic, an endless string of shopping malls. In the front seat his daughter turned around to see how he was bearing up.

They had decided to get off the Inland Island Highway and drive through Parksville because they knew the old man had lived there as a boy. On the outskirts of the town, traffic slowed to funnel into a single lane to cross over the Englishman River. Right there, upriver on that outcropping of rock, he had stood to cast out into the river for his first steelhead. As the car passed over the bridge, he closed his eyes and saw a rush of random images: blackberry runners crept out onto the edge of a dirt road, green-as-a-sapling new needles broke from the brown buds of the fir trees, mystical tidal pools lay in the bay where they gathered clams and oysters, yellow jackets swarmed the small trout drying in the sun on the pebbled shore. The push and shove of the sea in a twelve-foot clinker rowboat.

His daughter, looking back from the front seat, saw that he was sleeping and shook him awake. "Welcome to modern times, Dad."

He opened his eyes. The area where he had once run wild and free as a boy below the village, on miles of grassland that ended at the sea, was now filled with RVs and mobile homes. The owners had gathered there from all over the continent. They were encamped on the flatland at the edge of the sea, waiting for what? For the sky to open? No, in the end, the only way you could feel free was to be on a boat. In the end, that was all he knew.

"WAKE ME WHEN we get to Kelsey Bay," he said. His white-haired head slumped into his chest as he faded into sleep, dozing to the hiss of tires on hot summer pavement. Past the pulp mills north of Campbell River, the highway became a road lined with second-growth Douglas fir and a few cedar shake and shingle mills. Half an hour later, they turned off at the exit to Sayward, the road ending at the dock in Kelsey Bay.

"Where are we?" demanded the children, lost without the road signs of familiar franchises.

"Just beyond the northern end of Seymour Narrows," the old man said, suddenly awake and alert. "But that's not why we're here."

He was out of the car and walking down the dock before anyone could respond.

"Just leave him be," his daughter said. "The doctor told me half the time he doesn't know where he is anyhow."

"Well, he knew enough to insist on coming to Kelsey Bay."

Where was his ship? Had he come all this way for nothing? The light on the water was blinding, a metallic glare that shone like a sheet of crinkled aluminum foil stretched to the far horizon.

With his hand he shaded his eyes from the reflection but saw only indistinct blurred shapes, a log boom and beyond, a barge.

Then he realized what he was looking at. They had torn her apart for scrap in Victoria and towed the empty hull to Kelsey Bay. All that was left of the beautiful ship that had been his home for twenty-eight years, the ship they had polished and painted and run with pride, the flagship of the fleet, was an empty, listing hull, bleeding rust out of blistered paint.

This is how it ends, he thought, and reaching inside his jacket pocket removed some papers sealed in oilcloth. He slowly began unfolding the Seaman's Discharge Record Book that Boyce had given him so long ago, on the night he left the *Cardena* in a small boat with a father he didn't know.

There was a whole life written in his discharge papers, from the few days of his first voyage to the record of the years he had served onboard the *Cardena,* all neatly delineated in columns under headings: Name of Ship, Date and Place of Engagement/Discharge, Description of Voyage, Report of Character, Ability, General Conduct, and, in the final column, under Signature of Master of the Ship, Boyce's initials, the columns filled with the memory of those years on the *Cardena.*

He couldn't bear to look out into the bay at the ship's last rusting remains and his gaze dropped to the water swirling by the dock. Suddenly, he didn't know why, he was tearing his discharge book into small scraps of paper that were carried away in the current the instant they touched the water.

Memories flooded in on him as fast as the tidal stream ripping through the Narrows. It was in the Narrows that Grayson had sent him up the mast in a bosun's chair and Boyce had stalled the ship in the full flood of the tide.

Voices carried across the water and mingled with the cries of gulls and the sound of the sea lapping against the dock pilings below him. Though he was the only person on the dock he heard the voices of families waiting for the weekly arrival of the *Cardena.*

Boat Day. People waving and shouting greetings. Passengers lining the rails of the ship, calling out greetings, looking for friends, giving and receiving news.

In 1949 the Union steamships carried half a million passengers. Ten years later the red-and-black funnelled ships were gone forever and the ports of call themselves had disappeared: forty general stores, forty post offices, a dozen sawmills, five hospitals.

He thought about the woman with the dog he had met on

the dock in Vancouver on the night they boarded the *Cardena*. Fifteen years later, when Matt was thirty, she had died. Many times, when he was ashore in Vancouver, he had gone to the art gallery to view her paintings, trying to understand them. Gradually he came to realize that she was not painting trees but her relationship with trees.

"WHERE'S GRAMPS?" CHORUSED the children.

"A minute ago he was standing down there at the end of that dock. Now he's not there. Where's your dad?" the man asked his wife.

"Oh my God! You don't think . . ."

They bolted out of the car and hurried down the ramp onto the dock, the children running behind them. "Gramps!"

But the old man was nowhere in sight. There was no one on the dock itself, though people were onboard some of the boats tied to it.

"What's going on?" A man poked his head out of the hatch of his sailboat.

"Have you seen a very old man?"

"No. I was asleep before you folks started yelling."

The head disappeared, the hatch slammed shut. They looked at each other in panic. "We never should have . . ."

They began pacing. "He was standing right here at the end of the dock."

They looked down into the water below; it was dark, deep enough to drown in. A few scraps of torn paper that hadn't been carried away floated on the surface.

At the end of the dock, apart from the other boats, a small, badly listing troller leaned into the pier. Accumulated disorder cluttered a deck crammed with turnbuckles, rope, fuel cans, and a rusting anchor lashed to the base of the mast. There was no name on the bow. A mottled mixture of colours had been painted on it over the years, small square patches of tin and cloth soaked in tar tapped and squeezed into a leaking hull. From inside, voices emanated.

"There's someone inside. I hear voices," Matthew's daughter said.

But as soon as she said this, the voices inside the boat ceased, as if they did not wish to be heard.

Below the waterline, seaweed clung to the hull, trailing a lazy length of green. On deck a row of polished lures hung on their hooks from a wire. They flashed in the sun as they spun on swivels, tinkling in the light breeze like wind chimes.

On the forward deck the bald head of a man emerged as he climbed out of the fo'c'sle hatch. He stepped onto the deck and shuffled toward the stern in rolled-down rubber boots and a stained Stanfield undershirt. He was trying to reach the stern line wrapped around the cleat on the wharf.

"Say, son, can you undo that line on the dock for me? We're about to shove off for the Narrows."

"Look! There's Gramps!"

The old man was coming out of the fo'c'sle hatch holding a tin mug, which he set down on the deck. He quickly moved to release the forward line. They had never seen him so animated.

"Dad!" It was his daughter. "Get off that boat this instant! Immediately!"

He sat on the bulwarks, not moving, and stared stubbornly at her. Why did she insist on always talking to him as if he were a child?

The gentle undulations of the Pacific bumped the sides of the battered boat. He was so close now he could touch it, feel it. He reached over the side and the warm water coursed through his fingers. He wasn't getting off. He wasn't going back. Ever.

LATER THAT DAY, at the south end of Seymour Narrows, the boats were waiting in coves and pockets for the south-flowing flood to diminish. Suddenly, leaning hard in the current, first one way, then the other, a strange-looking craft came through the gap. The waiting vessels watched it struggle to maintain control before it passed quickly by them.

EPILOGUE

THE PHOTOGRAPH OF EMILY CARR and her dog, taken dock-side, is held today in the archives of the University of British Columbia.

The pages of Emily's sketchbook that Matt glimpsed briefly on the *Cardena* have yellowed with age, become brittle and fragile, crumble to the touch, and are stored in dust-proof boxes in the British Columbia Archives.

Less than a year after her trip to Quatsino, Emily exhibited, with the Group of Seven in Toronto, her masterpiece, *Red Cedar*.

The *Catala*, the *Cardena*'s sistership, sank off Grays Harbor in Washington State.

ACKNOWLEDGMENTS

THE AUTHOR ACKNOWLEDGES AND IS indebted to the following works: *Whistle Up the Inlet*, Gerald Rushton; *Union Steamships Remembered*, Art Twigg; *The Good Company, an Affectionate History of the Union Steamships*, Tom Henry. Doris Shadbolt's *Seven Journeys, the Sketchbooks of Emily Carr* provides a description of the artist's 1930 journey on the *Cardena* and her trip to the villages of Quatsino Sound, as well as reproductions of actual pages from Emily Carr's sketchbook.

Susan Buss, research librarian, Vancouver Maritime Museum, provided access to Union Steamship documents.

Thanks to the following for reading early drafts and providing suggestions and encouragement:

Lynne Ellen Dagg

Lori Dagg

Dan Griffith

Gayla Reid

Danni Tribe

Gloria Cranmer Webster

Special thanks to David Yett and Andrew Carhartt for their technical assistance.

MEL DAGG is the author of three short story collections, *Four Wheel Drift: Stories New and Selected*, *Same Truck, Different Driver*, and *Women on the Bridge*. Born and raised on the West Coast, he has lived and worked in many parts of Canada as a teacher and technical writer, and has a PHD in Canadian literature from the University of New Brunswick. As a young man he worked on the famous ocean-going towboat *Lloyd B Gore*. He and his wife currently divide their time between Mexico and Vancouver Island. *Passage on the Cardena* is Mel's first novel.